I0521320

Storylandia

The Wapshott Journal
of Fiction

Issue 21

The Wapshott Press

Storylandia, Issue 21, The Wapshott Journal of Fiction, ISSN 1947-5349, ISBN 978-1-942007-12-8, is published at intervals by the Wapshott Press, now a 501(c)(3) nonprofit, PO Box 31513, Los Angeles, California, 90031-0513, telephone 323-201-7147. All correspondence can be sent to The Wapshott Press, PO Box 31513, LA CA 90031-0513. Visit our website at www.WapshottPress.org to learn more. This work is copyright © 2017 by Storylandia. The Wapshott Journal of Fiction, Los Angeles, California. Copyright © 2017 Bob Carlton and is reprinted here with the copyright owner's permission.

Storylandia is always seeking quality original short stories, novelettes, and novellas. Please have a look at our submission guidelines at www.Storylandia.WapshottPress.org or email the editor at editor@wapshottpress.org

Many thanks to editor Kathleen Bonagofsky for the proofread and editorial support.

Cover: "View from Maricopa Mountain near the Rio Gila," by Henry Cheever Pratt, oil on canvas, 1855 (http://bit. ly/2lx231m)

Storylandia

The Wapshott Journal of Fiction

Founded in 2009

Issue 21, Spring 2017

Edited by Ginger Mayerson

Table of Contents

Alias Chicken Smith

By Bob Carlton

Alias Chicken Smith

I

He's got pluck.
Sure does...pluck.
Yeah, pluck, like a chicken.
Haw Haw
Guffaw Guffaw
What's your name, son?
Smith he lied.
Smith...Chicken Smith. Well boys, we got us a
blacksmith, a silversmith, and a gunsmith. And now
we got us a chickensmith. Haw Haw

The origin myth, preserved in the
notes, apparently taken while playing
poker at the Rusty Pick Saloon, by
Penwick Gathright, founder, editor,
and publisher of the *Silvercliff Bugle*.
Never developed into an article so far
as anyone is able to ascertain. Odd,
given Gathright's later fascination
with the exploits of the notorious
badman.

II

A thought confounds me—what if men are not what they always do, but rather always do what they are?

What if I write everything I have ever done, and it ends up explaining nothing?

What if a man is not the sum of his acts? His acts only some of what he is?

Found in a leather-bound notebook, on the first page of which is an apparent title, "The True Account of the Life and Exploits of the Much-Maligned and Misunderstood Outlaw, Chicken Smith, as Written by Himself." There appear to have been several other proposed titles, all of which were blotted out. If any of this memoir was written, its whereabouts are unknown. Aside from the title page and this note, the entire notebook is blank.

III

Of his final resting place, we know this much: he lies in a plot at the Oakpark Memorial Cemetery in Silvercliff, Arizona, next to his wife, Marisol. A small, plain, upright stone marks the spot. On it is carved the following inscription:

BARNABUS CHANTWELL
1860-Aug. 6, 1945

The only mention of his death ran, fittingly enough, in the *Silvercliff Bugle*, where more momentous events relegated this news to the back page: "We also note the passing yesterday of saloon keeper Barney Chantwell, the man who was once better known as infamous local outlaw Chicken Smith." This tantalizing item is the first mention of Smith's real identity.

Biography

The most extensive biographical sketch, quoted in full below, is found in *The Encyclopedia of Shootists,* by Wes Carroll, Blue Frontier Press, 1978, where he sits immortalized between Bill Smith and Jack Smith. Though he merits mention in a handful of other secondary sources, with one minor exception, none contain any information that cannot be found in Carroll.

The lone exception can be found in the four paragraphs devoted to him in *Showdown at Dawn*, by Clancy Yeager, also from Blue Frontier Press, 1989. There is made the assertion, which is not borne out by any of the sources cited by Yeager, that "Smith, while on a self-imposed 'vision-quest' in southwest Texas, encountered the great Mescalero Apache warrior-chief Alsate, headed for Mexico with a herd of stolen ponies." While entirely possible, given what is known of the outlaw's mercurial nature and the activities at the time of Alsate, it must be stressed that the episode remains conjectural, and is quite likely apocryphal.

Since the publication of Carroll's work, the papers of the Gathright family have become available to researchers. When Chester Gathright died in 1978 without issue, the extensive family archives passed to Chester's aunt, Caroline Gathright Adams, who sold them to the Harry Ransom Center, University of Texas, Austin. Among them are numerous letters from Smith to the family, as well as many additional references to him in documents written by the Gathrights. Should any intrepid researcher piece all of them together, it would no doubt enlarge our view of Smith's character, as well as possibly give some idea of what was going on in the "lost years."

Chicken Smith (1860-Aug. 6, 1945): Born Barnabus Chantwell, St. Louis, Missouri. Of his father, little is known outside of his name, Spencer Chantwell, and his service in the U.S. Army from 1856 to circa 1861. He may have died during the Civil War, or he may have simply abandoned his family. All that can be said with reasonable certainty is that Barnabus was raised from an early age, with his sister Collette (born

1858), by his mother, Penelope Chantwell, and her spinster sister, Camellia Roberts. While little evidence for his upbringing remains, much can be inferred from a surviving letter written to him by his mother, and dated Feb. 27, 1875. The mere fact that it was found, carefully preserved among Smith's effects at the time of his death, is a clear indication of the close bond between mother and son. That she speaks to her teenage son, working as a cowhand on Chester Throckmorton's Lazy J Ranch in Texas, as one would to a reasonably well-educated adult certainly implies a level of schooling no doubt peculiar among his rusticated peers of the time. At any rate, it is from this letter that we learn that Smith was raised in St. Louis, where his presumably widowed mother and her unmarried sister supported themselves by taking in boarders. He and his sister Collette were very close, and it can be fairly surmised that her tragic death by drowning in the Mississippi River, an apparent suicide resulting from a romantic disappointment, had the effect of setting Smith, then aged thirteen, on his way southwest. Within a year he was in the employ of Throckmorton, who noted the fact that his new ranch hand, though slight of stature and beardless of chin, was a quick study, a hard worker, and utterly fearless. It is this combination of a disciplined intelligence and physical courage that many people would remember most about him. It soon became apparent that he also possessed a manual dexterity and hand-eye coordination that few of his contemporaries could match. He quickly became a crack shot with a quick draw. This stood him in good stead with Throckmorton until he left off driving cattle after arriving in Ellsworth, Kansas, in 1876. It is at this point that Barnabus Chantwell exits the stage of history, not to re-enter until some thirty-five years later. His whereabouts and activities from this time until his arrival, in 1880, in the mining town of Silvercliff, Arizona, where he assumed the sobriquet by which he is best known, are a matter of conjecture. There is the intriguing possibility, based on the recollections of an Indian warrior named Broken Fang, that Smith was living among a band of Cheyenne during at least part of this period. Why Smith came to Silvercliff in the first place is something of a mystery, since he appears never to have engaged in any activities related to mining, gambling, pandering, or law enforcement. At any rate, his first known altercation that involved gun-play occurred soon after his arrival. It would seem that Smith, always slight of build and youthful in appearance, often bore the brunt of the crude and drunken jokes that tended to run rampant in a rough and tumble mining town. While most who met him described him as a quiet man, given to melancholy, and slow to anger, he was known, when sufficiently prodded, to display a caustic wit that would almost invariably provoke physical violence in those who were not equipped with the intellect to answer him. Such appears to be the case when miner Calvin Jenkins drew down on him in the Rusty Pick Saloon on May 17, 1880. Smith dove for cover behind a table as the inebriated Jenkins fired off two wild shots, one hitting the ceiling, the other grazing the arm of a prostitute named Gloria. Meanwhile, Smith had unholstered his Colt, and quickly fired two shots of his own. The first hit Jenkins in the right shoulder, the second splintered a nearby wooden support beam, a sliver of which caught Jenkins in the right eye. Though he would recover from his wounds, Jenkins would never be able to fire a pistol again and wore an eye patch for the rest of his life. Smith's outlaw status was confirmed when, the next day, Sheriff Townes Marshall and a group of citizens deputized for the occasion attempted to apprehend Smith. It was well-known that Marshall was a good friend of Jenkins, and that his "deputies" were little more than drunken rabble bent on causing Smith bodily harm. Smith, barricaded in a stable where he boarded his horse, held the posse to a stand-off for seventeen hours, aided, it is said, by the same prostitute Jenkins had shot. At the first opportunity, when many of the participants on the sheriff's side had either gone home, went for liquor, or gone to sleep, Smith galloped out of town and into the Arizona countryside. History has not recorded the fate of the prostitute Gloria. Following this embarrassing episode, Sheriff Marshall began his pursuit of Smith, largely by way of what would today be called propaganda. It seems there was no criminal act committed throughout Silvercliff and environs that did not feature Chicken Smith. While Penwick Gathright, a political foe of the sheriff and editor of the *Silvercliff Bugle*, exposed Marshall's tactics through his satirical coverage of Smith's exploits, he simultaneously, and perhaps unwittingly, grew the outlaw's legend as well. Some of Gathright's more unsophisticated readers may even have taken much of what he wrote at face value. Smith's popularity reached its peak in 1889, with the publication of *The Blazing Guns of Chicken Smith* by Garrett Hartley. Essentially a dime novel masquerading as biography, it can safely be said of it that not a single kernel of truth rests amidst Hartley's western-fringed purple prose. While Sheriff Marshall's accusations against Smith were largely unfounded, the outlaw did seem to support himself, at least in some measure, by larceny at the expense of the sheriff and his close supporters. Such would have been the case during the daytime robbery of the Silvercliff Savings and Loan, the president of which, John "Crying Jack" Stanton, was a close friend of Sheriff Marshall. Smith, who was never a man to court attention, rode unnoticed into town on June 16, 1882, and entered the bank alone. Having caught employees and customers alike by surprise with his brazenness, Smith quickly cleaned out the vault. A verbal altercation arose between Smith and one Clem Wiggins, during which an enraged Wiggins attempted to pull a small Derringer hidden in his cummerbund, only to have two of his fingers blown off by Smith. In the ensuing panic, Smith made off with roughly $15,000. While no one who was present doubted that the Silvercliff robbery was Smith's work, and certainly worthy of a long prison term, for some reason Sheriff Marshall felt it necessary to implicate Smith in a stage hold-up that same day near Standish Wells, in which a group of four masked highwayman killed the driver and a guard before robbing the passengers. The fact that Standish Wells was a two hour ride from Silvercliff and the two robberies were committed only thirty minutes apart cast doubt on all sides. In fact, between Sheriff Marshall's overzealous manufacturing of Smith's criminal acts and the *Silvercliff Bugle*'s lampooning of the same, much of the local citizenry either saw Marshall as a buffoon, Smith as a hero, or both. The only other incident of gun-play involving Chicken Smith for which we have primary documentation occurred Oct. 7, 1883, near the home of a sheriff's deputy named Tiberius Lee. It seems Smith had ridden with all due stealth onto Lee's property that morning with the apparent intent of stealing some chickens. The commotion of such an activity roused Lee from slumber, whereupon he appeared on his front porch brandishing a shotgun. Still half-asleep and possibly half-drunk as well, Lee fired wildly in Smith's general direction, causing little damage beyond blowing several of his own chickens to bits. Smith wheeled his horse around and fled, firing his pistol over his shoulder in Lee's general direction to cover himself as he fled. Lee stepped off the porch and prepared to fire again. In so doing, he tripped and fell, his shotgun discharging into his left foot, with the result that he lost several toes. This incident is the basis for the most well-known of the Chicken Smith legends, in which he fires his pistol over his shoulder from a galloping horse with such preternatural accuracy that he incapacitates his foe and picks off half the man's livestock at the same time. Both the *Silvercliff Bugle* and Hartley recount the event, and both make for wonderful comedy, the former piece intentionally, the latter not so much. Finally, in November, Sheriff Marshall was able to apprehend Smith. Acting on a tip from an informant, Marshall found Smith playing cards at Green's No. 6 Saloon. Seeing that the Sheriff, accompanied by several cohorts, had the drop on him, Smith surrendered without incident. Justice at the local level being what it was at the time, the outlook for Smith was not good. However, Penwick Gathright secured the services of noted attorney and former federal prosecutor for the Territory, Clifford Bunting. Bunting argued before a county judge that one of the crimes of which Smith was accused, namely the shooting of Tiberius Lee, actually occurred outside the county, and should therefore be tried in a different venue. Because of the political influence of Gathright and Bunting, Smith was removed from Sheriff Marshall's custody by the rather intimidating Deputy Federal Marshal Jake "Stand Alone" Allenby, and transferred to a jail in Cullahoolah, from which he promptly escaped, but not before trying his case in the press in a jailhouse interview with the *Silvercliff Bugle*. It might be pertinent at this point to address the question of why Penwick Gathright, a respected businessman, civic leader, and law-abiding citizen would take such a personal interest in the fate of an outlaw, even one who provided such good copy. Some have seen Gathright's interest in Smith as politically motivated. In this view, Smith is little more than a pawn used by Gathright and his friends to further their agenda against Sheriff Marshall, the mining interests, and the corrupt political machine they had assembled. However, it makes little sense given the amount of personal expense, as well as exposure to physical danger, to which Gathright put himself. The matter became clarified by way of the author's personal correspondence with Chester Gathright, the grandson of Penwick Gathright. It seems that in July, 1882, a fire broke out at an abandoned miner's shack on the edge of town. Several boys had been playing in it, and one, Granville Gathright, the nine-year-old son of Penwick Gathright, was trapped inside. As luck, or fate, would have it, Chicken Smith was in the vicinity and heard the shouts of the boys for help. At the risk of his own life, Smith rescued young Granville, receiving a severe burn on his left upper-arm which left a distinctive scar, one which he was able to conceal, but which was known to the Gathright family. The grateful father would ever after help Smith in any way he could, or in any way the latter would allow. This included favorable press, paid legal expenses, and possible assistance in the Cullahoolah jailbreak. This familial debt was honored through three generations, discharged only upon the death of Smith himself. At any rate, after escaping from jail, Smith essentially vanished. Beginning in 1884, there is not a single credible source which makes any mention of him. This is all the more remarkable since, from approximately 1885 to 1899, Smith is constantly making his movements public by way of communication with the *Silvercliff Bugle*. He is almost like a traveling correspondent, sending his posts from all across the United States. His letters to the paper continued to fuel the old rivalries between Gathright and his opponents, as Smith's continued freedom became symbolic of the latter's incompetence. The fact that Smith remained remarkably well-informed on the constantly shifting political landscape of Silvercliff suggests either regular communication with Gathright, which is highly unlikely given Smith's peripatetic lifestyle, or more likely, a conscious effort by Smith to keep up with current events. Whatever the case may be, Smith's continued presence in the civic life of Silvercliff cemented his local legend and, it may even be plausibly argued, helped pave the way for the land and banking reforms that saved Silvercliff from the fate of other mining boomtowns of the era. It may not be overstating the case too much to say that Penwick Gathright and Chicken Smith are the fathers of modern Silvercliff. Beginning in 1899, there is once more a gap in what we know of the life of Chicken Smith. Where he was and what he was doing are a matter of pure conjecture. All that can be said with certainty is that by 1911, Chicken Smith had once again become Barnabus Chantwell. He returned to Silvercliff, where he resided in anonymity. With the exception of Penwick and Granville Gathright, most old friends and foes had either died or moved away. He purchased the now-defunct Rusty Pick Saloon and reopened it as the Second Chance Saloon. In March of that year, at age 51, he had married Marisol Castillo, age 24. Little is known of his wife; she was the daughter of a Mexican army officer and a woman named Pilar, formerly a captive of Apaches. Marisol herself seems to have been raised in a convent near the Texas-Mexico border after the death of her father, Capt. Manuel Castillo, when she was an infant. It is believed Smith met her here, and that the two of them decided to start a new life together. His domestic bliss was short-lived however, when his wife died two years later giving birth to a stillborn son. From this point forward, there are mainly passing references to Chantwell in the *Silvercliff Bugle*, usually in connection to his presence or participation in some civic function. His later life seems to have been quiet and uneventful until a hot July evening in 1938, when a fight broke out in his saloon. A local tough named Benny Compton, drunk and belligerent, attacked another man, Stanley Thursby. At almost the same moment that a knife appeared in Compton's hand a shot rang out, and Compton immediately dropped to his knees, clutching his bloody right forearm. Everyone in the crowded bar turned to see old Barney Chantwell, holding a Colt pistol in one hand and dialing the phone to call the police with the other. Witnesses later marveled at the lightning-fast speed with which the entire incident occurred, and the calm, steady, almost serene manner of the old bartender. The last time Chicken Smith is known to have handled a gun he was no longer even known as Chicken Smith. Barnabus Chantwell died at the age of 85, on Aug. 6, 1945, in Silvercliff, Arizona, a well-liked and respected businessman.

Chicken Smith's reputation, that of a feared gunfighter and desperado, would appear to be largely unfounded. The incidents of gun-play in which he was a known participant were largely drunken, sloppy affairs. As far as we know, he was never responsible for taking a single human life. The crimes which earned him outlaw status seem to have been largely fabricated, or at the very least grossly exaggerated, by authorities whose own behavior was often legally questionable. However, we would do well to remember that not many legends stand up under close scrutiny. Some few will weather the revisions of history. Wyatt Earp, Wes Hardin, and Bill Hickock retain their near-mythic status, even when cut down to size. The same can be said of Chicken Smith. He was physically courageous and fiercely loyal to his friends. His speed and accuracy with a gun were combined with a coolness of temper that no doubt contributed to extending his life. His wit and intelligence could both serve him well and get him in trouble. For whatever reason, he seems to have formed an attachment to Silvercliff, and in his own strange fashion, in alliance with the Gathright family, sought to strengthen his community and wrest it away from those he saw as corrupted by the prospect of easy fortune at the expense of their fellow citizens. While he was certainly no Robin Hood, Chicken Smith, with the help of Penwick Gathright, was nonetheless seen by many readers of the *Silvercliff Bugle* as a crusader for social justice. Even while on the run from 1885 to 1911, he continued to assist his friends from afar in their political battles. His contribution to the history of the West, in comparison to the other figures in this volume, is thus utterly unique, for his influence on the fate of a particular place was much more far-reaching and nuanced than that of almost any of his more celebrated contemporaries.

Primary Sources,
with Commentary as Needed,
Interspersed with Occasional Prose

Note: Those sources preceded by '*' are the primary documents used by Wes Carroll in his biographical sketch of Chicken Smith found in *The Encyclopedia of Shootists*. More recently discovered documents unavailable to Carroll have been inserted where it seemed most appropriate.

* * *

*Letter: Penelope Chantwell to her son, Barnabus, Feb. 27, 1875

My Dearest Son,

I hope this letter finds you at Mr. Throckmorton's, though I know not when you will be on the trail. Additionally, I hope it finds you doing well. Your Aunt Camellia sends you her kindest regards. I apologize for not writing more often, but as I am sure you can well imagine, we are very busy here at the house—we have taken two new boarders just this past week. Both are young men, though of course we were vigilant in the matter of their references. They are both starting out in their professions, one in the law and one in the practice of medicine. While not so young as yourself, their presence here gives me a melancholy turn now and again, for they remind me of you, and the life you might have had. I know very well the pain you have felt for the last two years, the suffering you have known since the Mississippi—which I must look upon daily!—took away our dear Collette. That Love should thus treat an innocent so is a Mystery that I suppose you and I have had to treat in our own separate fashions. Though I mourn your absence daily, I also pray that you find some way in your travels that will lead to the comfort of your soul. I know you have turned away from the simple tenets of our Faith, and for that I cannot blame you. I have myself put God on trial in the night, and for that indignity to His ways I may someday have to answer. We all, I suppose, must come to our own Natural Religion. For myself, at my age, I shall no doubt creep back into the belief that God's will be done, and Justice served on the Day of Judgment. Though it may be vain comfort, it is comfort nonetheless. What matters the anodyne to one in torment?

I apologize, dear Barnabus, if this missive has been to this point nothing but bleak. As you know me, I may have my darker moments, but I am seldom morose. This is, I think, a thing we share. You have your dear father's eyes, his quick grace, and long, fine limbs—but we share an inward gazing eye that he never had, God bless him—whether fallen on some battlefield or in some New Orleans pleasure house. Please forgive the vulgarities of your sometimes bitter mother! Ha ha! Our laughter, son, is never far removed from our rages and pains. This is how I know you will always make it through. Even your blackest moods draw forth your wit. It is our shield against the darkness. Poor Collette—she had the darkness only.

It is certain that sometimes I fear for you son, especially when you first left—at such a tender age and from the only home you had ever known. But your every letter increases both my pride and my certainty of your ability to hold your own, as they say. Placate my future fears at your earliest opportunity.

Love,

Mother

P.S. I am sending along by separate post a volume of verse by Lazarus, a friend of Emerson, whose work I know you have long enjoyed.

The book by Emma Lazarus, probably *Admetus and other poems,* was not found among Smith's papers after his death. Perhaps he never received it. He was, however, known to be familiar with her work, at least according to Chester Gathright in a radio interview from 1948.

# # #

*KACS Radio Interview with Chester Gathright, March 1948.

Question: So Smith was a well-read man then?

Chester Gathright: Oh, very much so. I don't know where he was educated, or to what extent he was conventionally schooled. I do know that his mother imparted a great deal of learning to him. She seemed to have impressed upon him the value of some sort of education.

Q: Do you know the kinds of things he liked to read? I understand that a handful of books were found after his death.

CG: Well, it's hard for me to say. I mean, I only got to know him after he came back to Silvercliff in, oh, I guess it was 1911 or so. So I only really knew him as Barney Chantwell, saloon keeper. What his interests were thirty years earlier I don't know. There is the letter we have from his mother that mentions sending him the Lazarus book...

Q: Emma Lazarus, correct?

CG: Yes, that's right. He was apparently very familiar with her work. I can remember once when my father and I visited him at home. It must have been shortly after his wife passed away...

Q: And she died during childbirth, did she not?

CG: Yes. That actually relates to this story. His wife, Marisol, died while giving birth to a son, who was stillborn. Not a terribly uncommon occurrence at the time, but still very tragic, very sad. And I remember seeing him, I must have been about ten or so at the time, and he and my father were talking—I think we were in the parlor of Chantwell's house. At any rate, they had reached a sort of lull in the conversation. I remember having the impression they were wrapping things up at that point. So after a brief silence, Barney takes a sip of his drink, iced tea, or so I thought, maybe something stronger, I don't know, and then he says, "The funeral and the marriage, now, alas! / We know not which is sadder to recall." It was like he was summing up the whole event and that was the end of it. It was several years later that I found out he was quoting the Emma Lazarus poem about the deserted synagogue, which she wrote when she was a teenager, if I recall.

Q: So do you think he had read it right after it was published, what, thirty or forty years earlier, or read it much later? I mean, did he seem to have that kind of recall, that he could freely quote an apropos passage of verse he had not read in years, or would it have been something he had read recently, to match the occasion?

CG: Interesting question, but I really don't know. From what I can remember of his conversation, he seemed to use literary quotations as a kind of box for his feelings, like he could relate what he felt to an aphoristic sort of passage. It was almost like he was objectifying his emotions, putting them into, like I say, a box, a box made out of someone else's words.

He but broods and reads, out among the coyotes and crows. Lowing cattle, crickets singing in natural meter, awaken articulations no words of his own can capture.

# # #

Poems, Mary Tucker, 1867

This heavily-marked volume was among the books found after Barnabus Chantwell's death. Chantwell's annotations take the form of underlined passages with a date noted in the margin. This practice appears to remain consistent throughout his life. The earliest example is dated "June? 1871", from a poem entitled "Little Bell":

> Years of joy cannot redeem us
> As a nation from disgrace.
> (p. 75)

The last marked passage is dated
January 23, 1943:

> I must get some coffee—beg borrow or steal—
> For after that Java, I can't drink parched meal!
> ("Upon Receipt of a Pound of
> Coffee in 1863" p. 107)

The first two underlined quotations
below bear the date April 4, 1873. The
third is dated October 12, 1874, when
he would have presumably been on the
trail with a herd of Throckmorton's
cattle.

> He charmed my heart with some unholy spell,
> He was a serpent, whom I loved so well.
> ("The Blight of Love" p. 15)

> And the maiden's heart was broken.
> ("Only a Blush" p. 79)

> Avaunt, dark image of despair!
> Why dost thou still go raving?
> ("The First Gray Hair" p. 8)

It may seem strange that a man of
Chantwell's intelligence and ironic
melancholy would find such value in
the clumsy rhythms and easy religious
sentimentality of this daughter of the
South. However, in examining those
passages which he marked, one can see
that Chantwell is appropriating bits
and pieces out of context to reflect

his own moods. The third instance quoted is a good example. The poem itself, which appears early in the volume, is a meditation on aging; thirteen-year-old Chantwell picks out two lines that resonate with him, but for presumably a very different reason than that of the poet. While we cannot be absolutely certain that he notes them in response to his continued grief at his sister's death, there does not appear to be another emotional crisis in his life at this time which would have provoked such a response.

He dates each revelation, as if an outline of his spiritual progress could be drawn up, the private history of his soul reconstituted, the brandy of the poet's words turned back into the wine of his life.

\# \# \#

From Pride of Place: A Memoir, by Chester Throckmorton. Reprinted by Farthest West Press, 1962.

The first herd of the spring [March 1874—Ed.] was already on the trail. I had a smaller herd, no more than 1500 head, that I wished to drive north that summer, hoping thus to arrive in Ellsworth before the first hard frost. As such, I began taking on new hands almost immediately after the year's first departure. Many of these young men had been with me before, and most had some experience punching cattle. Among them was Calvin Thurman, who would, over the course of the next decade, prove himself competent to such a degree that he would one day replace my long time foreman, Bud Stanwyck. As always, there were a few greenhorns, some of whom could not adapt to life on the trail, some of whom took to it almost immediately. I remember, as an example of the latter, one Barney Chatwell [sic], who came, if I recollect correctly, from St. Louis. He stands out in my mind for his youth and small size. He looked to be barely weened, but this appearance was quite deceptive. I had never met one so young who had this boy's drive to master whatever task was given him. Smart as a whip, he could instantly grasp what any job required of him, both physically and mentally. He could throw himself into any situation with a perfect courage. He seemed certain of his own capacities, much more so than most men twice his age. I remember more than once remarking that if I had a dozen more like him, within a very few years I would be operating a ranch that ran with an almost military precision.

# # #

*From KACS Radio Interview with Chester Gathright, March 1948

Question: I know we've talked a good deal about Smith's, what?, more intellectual side? But he was no doubt a tough customer as well, was he not? I mean, to have lived the life he did, and survive as long as he did, I mean, we are not talking about just some effete school boy here are we?
Chester Gathright: No, not at all. I mean, of course

not. Like I've said before, his more notorious days were before I came along. But let me just say first off, that from personal experience, when I was old enough to get to know him well and frequent his saloon, he always struck me as a man you simply did not start trouble with. He just commanded respect. There was seldom a disturbance in his place. He just handled himself in such a cool and collected way, you could tell that he was not someone to cross. And remember, this is when he is sixty, seventy years old.

Q: So he was what? Physically intimidating? Gruff?

CG: No, no, not at all. As I say, cool and collected. If you've ever read my grandfather's memoirs...

Q: No, I have not.

CG: Well, then, in there you can see that his natural ability to control a situation goes back a long way. He always seemed very deliberate in what he did, even when acting on what you or I might see as the spur of the moment...

Q: But for him it wasn't? Spur of the moment, I mean?

CG: Exactly. It just seemed that his mind could calculate possibilities that fast. He was never reckless, even when acting instantaneously.

# # #

*From a Letter, Jess Caldwell to his sister, Beth Ann, 1886

Recollect I once worked with a kid name of Barney Cantwell [sic], back when I was riding point for Throckmorton. Never seen a man with quicker mind or quicker hands and he couldn't been more than twelve.

I guess he must have been, but he sure didn't look it. Anyhow, I was learning him how to use a handgun— he had a nice Colt as I remember, not new, but well kept. Gave him a few pointers and next I know he's shooting cans off fence posts at twenty paces, drawing straight up, no aiming. Jesus, he was good.

# # #

*From *Blood and Ink: Memoir of a Frontier Newsman* by Penwick Gathright, posthumously published by Press Westward, 1931.

Chicken Smith was, quite simply, one of the most remarkable men I had ever met. He arrived in Silvercliff in 1880, barely twenty years old. I believe I can safely say that anyone who met him, whether friend or foe, would have found several traits in him worthy of emulation. I believe what most impressed me was his ability to face any given situation with a cool and detached judgment, which consequently resulted in choosing the appropriate course. His actions were always quick and decisive without ever being rash. His mental agility was perfectly matched by a physical grace and athleticism with which he was able to carry out any action he deemed necessary. His eyes directed what his hands accomplished. His movements were precise but never stiff, unhurried but always a step ahead of any opponent. His accuracy with a handgun was undisputed. He was, in short, exactly the kind of man one would welcome as a friend when facing a formidable opponent.

# # #

*From the *Swayback* [N.M.] *Post-Dispatch* article "Recollections of a Plains Indian Warrior" March 27, 1926

We wintered one year at the White Deer Agency when a band of Cheyenne passed through on their way south. We had not been at war with them since the time of my father's father. Traveling with them was a young white man. He was very thin and dark from the sun, like pemmican. They called him "Brownie," like the word in the white man's tongue. He spoke with them in Cheyenne, and they treated him as one of their own. It was plain to see he could come and go as he wished. He was not a prisoner. Mostly I remember him because I had never seen anyone who could shoot like him with a pistol. He would win money from soldiers at the agency. The other white men did not like him so much because he was Cheyenne, but the buffalo soldiers befriended him and laughed that he could outshoot any soldiers.

# # #

*Letter, Marty Prince to his mother, Sept. 22, 1874

Dear Ma,

I have been two days now in Ellsworth, and now that Mr. Throckmorton's bus[i]ness here is mostly ended, I have a few moments to [w]rite to you. I am sure you have probly [sic] heared [sic] wild tales of what goes on in "cowtown." Much is true, and much worse beside[s], but none as I would tell to you. How[e]ver, you will be glad to kno[w] that I have keep [sic] my wits about me and strayed away from

trubl [sic]. Mostly I stick with the boys of my outfit, like one kid name[d] Barnny [sic] Chancel [sic]. You would lik[e] him Ma—as steady as sunrise. I never seen a man as good with a gun, and he nev[e]r has to use it! None [of] these greasers can rile him—he just smile[s] and walk[s] a way, or frouns [sic] and they walk away. I know he would be a good man in a fight, so I keep close to him and the other Throckmorton gang. Anyhow Ma—I just want[e]d to let you know I was doin[g] good, and hop[e] to see you soon.
Love,
    Marty

# # #

*Diary of Blue-Jacket Qualls, entry for Sept. 29, 1876

We have arrived in Ellsworth. The boys got paid, and as is the custom, we have proceeded to give it all back. Days pass in the serious business of sport. Gambling, fighting, shooting, and loving—we re-filled the local coffers only recently emptied out to us. Finally, the day has come when, hung over and broke, we saddle up and head back home to Texas. Among our casualties this time out was Barny [sic] C'well, who has headed off more westerly than south, his pockets still lined with the larger part of his pay. We are all sorry to see him go. No better friend on the trail could be found, never minded riding drag with the greenhorns, never missed a shot he took, never took a shot in anger or in haste. Always quick with a joke, but slow and thoughtful with advice. Would do the lowest of chores without complaint, do the most taxing ones without mistake. A good hand.

# # #

*From Mary Tucker, *Poems*.

I waited for I know not what;
But, oh, I waited there,
Hoping, perchance, some ray to find,
To lighten my despair.

("The Tryst" p. 57)

Underlined passage, dated May 17, 1879.

He performs physical miracles with only the desert as witness. Vultures speak to him, the vast, involved grammar of decay. Lunatic reptiles whisper their night heresies into his daylight ears as he sleeps. A lone figure astride the dunes watches over him. From distant ridgelines shimmering in the heat amidst the ghosts of water he hears the cry of desert mice, the falling tears of hawks. He awakes back into history, speaking the secret language of a new guide and carrying a smooth glass bead given him by the lightning.

# # #

*From the *Silvercliff Bugle*, May 18, 1880

We are sad to report the injury last evening to one Calvin Jenkins during an unpleasant bit of gunplay at the Rusty Pick Saloon. Mr. Jenkins, we are told, is a member of that genteel tribe known as Miners. He apparently graduated from the Academy of Mere Prospecting, this advancement purportedly procured for him through the good offices of the Silvercliff Mining concern. It seems, however, that his social habits have remained largely unchanged despite his new station, for witnesses state that Mr. Jenkins, well into his revels, began harassing a young man sitting at the bar, who was by all accounts minding his own business. Apparently, the cultured witticisms of Jenkins provoked a verbal retort, whereupon Jenkins took offense at the insolence of the young desperado, whose nom de guerre, we have been told, is Chicken Smith. Though posterity does not record Smith's exact words, they seem to have inflamed the moral outrage of Jenkins, whose thunderous bellow was eclipsed by the reports of the two shots he fired. The only casualties were an unfortunate ceiling beam and the upper arm of one Gloria, whose wiles and charms, if not in excelsios, are still, so we are told, priced somewhat above the going rate, and well worth it given the return on investment, or so it is said. No doubt the local constabulary would agree, given that she is often found cuffed in their custody, though seldom under arrest.

Meanwhile, the young valiant, Smith, who had ducked behind an upset table for cover, emerged from hiding with his Colt a-blazing. His first shot caught Jenkins in the right shoulder, while a second shattered a wooden beam beside which the stricken warrior slumped. Misfortune for poor Jenkins abounded, as a splinter from the beam launched itself into his right eye. Smith escaped in the ensuing panic. Dr. Clement Stallings was summoned to the scene to treat the wounded. It is believed that the scratch on the arm of the fair maiden will have no adverse effect on her future business opportunities. As for the miner Jenkins, though his injuries do not appear to be life-threatening, it will probably be some time before our fair town can expect further displays of his verbal wit and expert marksmanship.

# # #

*From a Letter, Myra Dobbs to her son Gerald, Oct. 28, 1911

You will no doubt remember the name Calvin Jenkins, your father's uncle on his mother's side. He passed away last week at the age of sixty-one. He came to Tucson only about six months ago, and he was in a pretty bad way even then. Your father and I would help him out when we could, cooking for him, running errands, visiting several times a week. He was really a very interesting man, full of stories, though I think he was very sad and bitter in many ways. He had apparently lived a hard life his last thirty years, made hard for the most part by drink. However, when he came here he had given up the bottle, though the ravages of those years were easily enough seen. He still carried with him the scars, on both body and spirit, of his younger days as a prospector. I am sure you know the story told in your father's family of Uncle Calvin's shootout with the infamous badman Chicken Smith. It was always told with great pride and relish, polished and embellished over the years into a tale heroic or comic, depending on the occasion. Of course, most of the people doing the telling had never met him, or had not seen him in years. To me, he was more like a legend than a real man. Then one day, here he was, in the flesh. While Uncle Calvin had many funny and thrilling stories, he never talked of his showdown with Chicken Smith, at least not directly. You see, it was obvious that Uncle Calvin had got the worst of it. He could barely use his right arm, and he wore a patch over his right eye, which was either blind or missing. Though I am sure time had made him into the cripple I met, I have no doubt that his carousing days ended after the affair with Smith. His bitterness, though, seemed less directed at Smith than his former friends of the time. Uncle Calvin was apparently friends with some prominent people in that area, such as the sheriff and important people at one of the local mining companies. It seemed, at least to Uncle Calvin, that once he had served his purposes to them, they turned their backs on him, and he was forced to make his own way. As I say, these are my own thoughts, based on the impressions he gave me. I felt very bad for him, and secretly wished a bad end for Chicken Smith and his cronies. God knows Uncle Calvin had his faults, but the broken man I knew for the last six months was not deserving of the fate that befell him. I take comfort in the fact that, despite the continued bitterness at the turns his life had taken, at the end I think he was starting to accept the hand dealt to him, that despite the long pain his injuries and years of drinking gave him, he ended up a sober and upright man in the eyes of the Lord. I wanted to tell you all this Gerald so that when the story gets told and re-told, as it certainly will, you remember that Calvin Jenkins was a real man, who suffered real injuries and pain. He is a part of your family, Gerald, a part of your history, and not just a character in some other man's story.

#

*From the *Silvercliff Bugle,* May 20, 1880.

We have been apprised of further developments following the recent fracas at the Rusty Pick Saloon, wherein two of Silvercliff's leading citizens sustained considerable damage, outdone only by the injustices perpetrated against the august establishment itself. Sources familiar with the course of the entire tragedy inform us that yesterday morning, our county's stalwart sheriff, Townes Marshall, along with a group of perhaps a dozen or more civic-minded, law-abiding citizens, armed with badges newly-minted, whiskey well-aged, and guns never-fired, descended on Hal Brownwell's livery. The ostensible purpose of this well-oiled delegation to said stable was to disarm and arrest a notorious outlaw laid up therein, one Chicken Smith. While the majority of Silvercliff citizens seem to hold the opinion that Mr. Jenkins, lately shot up by the aforementioned Smith, "had it coming" as one man on the street put it, our Sheriff, holding the scales of blind Justice Herself ever before his eyes, was no doubt able to set aside his friendship with Mr. Jenkins, and their mutual ties (some might say "strings") to the Silvercliff Mining Company, in the interest of bringing this whole sad affair to an equitable conclusion.

Witnesses state that at approximately eight o'clock yesterday morning, the sheriff and his posse made their way to the stable to disarm Smith and demand his unconditional surrender. The sheriff's challenge was met with derisive laughter and gunshots from within. A lengthy stand-off, complete with curses, oaths, and sporadic gunfire, ensued. As the day wore on and the liquor wore off, tempers began to overtake the collective wisdom of the mob. A proposal was made, seconded, and heartily passed, to set fire to the structure. However, an impassioned appeal was made by Mr. Brownwell, with the assistance of a brandished shotgun, to spare his place of business. The addendum passed and the siege resumed in earnest. Sorties and feints were repelled by the defenders within, which included Smith and a certain soiled dove with wing recently clipped, who kept him steadily supplied with reloaded ordinance. Finally, the attackers apparently decided that Justice had been served but sufficient whiskey had not, with the result that by one o'clock this morning the triple goddesses Fatigue, Thirst, and Indifference colluded with Smith in his escape by horseback out the rear of the stable and into the welcoming desert. This afternoon, stable hand Jess Quinlan claims to have dug no less than one hundred twenty-two rounds out of the walls of the livery. It is indeed miraculous that the nefarious Chicken Smith was able to evade not only capture, but considerable loss of blood as well. We can only hope that our peace-loving community is well rid of him and can now rest safely in the hands of such men as Sheriff Townes Marshall, a man of proven integrity and, his price being set, well-established value.

# # #

*Letter, Sheriff Townes Marshall, to Gov. John Charles Fremont

From: Office of Sheriff Townes Marshall
Grant County, Arizona

To: The Honorable J.C. Fremont, Governor
Arizona Territory
Aug. 19, 1880

Dear Sir,

I feel it is my duty to inform you of the presence of an individual in the Territory that poses grave dang[e]r to its citizens. He goes by the name Chicken Smith, and is a most desprit [sic] and dangrus [sic] hard case. In the space of 3 months, he has terrized [sic] this county to the point that I beleave [sic] fed[e]ral interventi[o]n is necess[a]ry. He is a menace to all law[-a]biding people, [e]specially those in the country, such as farmers, ranchers, and prospecters [sic] who lie outside the city limits of our towns. He is known to have been involv[e]d in sev[e]r[a]l shootings, in some of which cases lives remain in the balance. His allies and cohorts infest the remote countryside, giving him aid and comfort even as they hinder our pursuit of him. It seems not a day goes by that a fresh crime cannot be added to his account. I apeel [sic] to you—if no manpow[e]r can be spar[e]d—please send funds so that adequate numbers of men can be deputiz[e]d so pursuit and capture may be affected.

# # #

*From the *Silvercliff Bugle,* Aug. 23, 1880.

It has come to our attention that in recent days, Sheriff Townes Marshall has formally appealed to the esteemed Governor of the Territory for federal assistance in the apprehension of that most infamous badman, Chicken Smith. As far as we have been able to ascertain, Smith's crime spree has resulted in over a dozen larcenies, numerous incidents of vandalism, and intimations of several murders, though according to Dr. Clement Stallings there have been no bodies turning up whose cause of demise has not been explained to the satisfaction of the authorities, to Smith's benefit.

It has become a joke among the small but formerly active guild of the criminal class that all are named Smith. It would appear that as long as Chicken Smith runs roughshod in the area, none need fear the drop of the judge's gavel or scaffold's trap door. We sincerely hope that the sheriff brings to a speedy conclusion this ugly chapter in our town's history, if for no other reason than to allow someone other than Chicken Smith to participate in the pursuit of ill-gotten gains.

# # #

*From the *Silvercliff Bugle,* Feb. 10, 1881

We regret to announce that due to the immense number of high crimes and misdemeanors perpetrated by Chicken Smith in the last twenty-four hours, the Silvercliff Bugle will not have enough room to print an account of all of them and still include such staples as birth and death announcements, or advertisements for the latest entertainments available at the Chanticleer. We apologize for any inconvenience incurred by the truncated version of his latest atrocities. While we are quite certain that Sheriff Marshall and his Myrmidons are doing their utmost to apprehend the miscreant, we sincerely hope on behalf of our subscribers and advertisers that the pursuit comes to a timely conclusion, for if this crime spree continues apace, we will be forced to raise our rates to cover the added expense of using more ink and paper to keep up with the course of events.

# # #

*From the *Silvercliff Bugle,* Feb. 19, 1879

In a recent census, it was determined that there were approximately 527 permanent residents in the town of Silvercliff. To serve the interests of those citizens, we have 18 saloons, 2 hotels, 6 cantinas, and 8 brothels (not including perhaps three or four "cat wagons" to service the outlying districts). In addition to the necessities of civilization, we have recently added a one-room schoolhouse and a new church, replacing the tent of former times since it can no longer hold any congregation above a dozen. That there may in fact be thirteen God-fearing people in our fair city is cause for celebration. Yet, with all the trappings of modern life, Silvercliff has, up to this point, stood bereft of a newspaper. The Silvercliff Bugle now endeavors to remedy this deficiency. Yet it is not merely for the purpose of disseminating news and information that we deem such an enterprise of urgent import. The simple fact is that the lack of knowledge concerning current events leaves the ignorant man prey to the designs of those who seek power and wealth through underhanded means. It is because such forces are at work among us now that the Bugle feels impelled to expose corruption to the plain sight of every citizen.

It is a sad fact that in our community, the municipal government is largely controlled by outsiders who seek to exploit the land and people of Grant County for personal gain. It is important to remember that Silvercliff came into being because of the rich local deposits of ore. While we may descry the personal conduct of the typical prospector when in town on a binge, the moral laxity of his behavior is as nothing compared to the large syndicates which seek, through money and influence, to deprive this pioneering individual of his hard-earned stake. It is the purpose of the Silvercliff Bugle to report on and condemn all such abuses of individual rights, by land grabbers, shady bankers, slick operators, crooked lawmen, open-palmed jurors, and all the rest whose practiced veneer of respectability cannot hide the stench of foul intentions. We look forward to the day when our stories consist of nothing more than the quotidian doings of a just society, but until then, we will not shirk what we feel is the duty incumbent upon us— that is, reformation through information.

# # #

*From *The Blazing Guns of Chicken Smith* by Garrett Hartley. Reprinted by Farther West Press, 1960.

Smith spurred his sable steed along the ridge that glowed softly in the vermillion light of sunset.

"My bonnie mount," he sang out jauntily, "what say we descend to yonder ravine and see if we may espy a suitable place to make our camp for the night?"

Suddenly, from out of the twilight, an arrow

whistled past his ear. Even before the red villain's war-cry had died away, Smith had spun about and fired, twin pistols spitting forth their lethal message into the darkness of a rocky outcropping in which Smith had determined on the instant that his assailant lay hidden. A moment of silence followed the echoes of Smith's messengers of death, whereupon a dark form tumbled from behind the rocks, rolled part way down the hill, and stopped, frozen in the awkward repose of his justly delivered fate.

"Requiescat in pace, fiendish rogue," spoke Smith, as his haughty stallion, unperturbed by the fatal commotion, daintily picked his way down the hillside to the secluded wash below.

# # #

*From the *Silvercliff Bugle,* Sept. 24, 1883

There is no mystery in explaining the source for both the origin and rapid growth of Silvercliff; it is contained within the name itself. While we do not necessarily endorse the more energetic behavior of prospectors when in town, it is due to their pioneering, individualistic spirit that any of us are camped in the middle of the Arizona desert. While we all descry the excesses of unbridled capitalism, make no mistake: whatever the dubious morality that inspired much of the commerce of Silvercliff, it has generally been done by the hands of individuals. Whatever the relative merits of attempting to get rich by digging up the earth or by picking the pocket of the person doing so, we have up until now always known that if we are being robbed, it is by our neighbor. No doubt heinous crimes are committed here every day, but when one prospector puts his pick ax through the skull of another over mining rights in a local cat house, it is an act that can be explained and understood, right then and there. Not so with the abuses perpetrated by those whose agenda is set from a distance, whose motives arise from afar, and whose agents work in unison to effect the purposes of a consortium without connection to the local community. Let us be clear on this point: the Silvercliff Mining Company is such an entity. The only reason for their presence in our town is to extract as much silver from the land as possible and siphon as much money from the locals as they can before absconding with the profits to more promising pastures. They do so with the active cooperation of those we have entrusted to look after our best interests, including our esteemed Sheriff Marshall and Justice of the Peace, the Honorable Franklin Moorehouse. While the Silvercliff Mining Company did not invent claim-jumping, they have raised it, as an art and science, to such a degree that it now appears a legitimate public institution. Evictions, writs of attachment, and redrawn city plots are the weapons of this class of criminal. Do not doubt the mailed fist lies just behind the shiny badge and notarized papers. Shipments of tools and supplies destined for the smaller local companies have been known to disappear into the countryside, hauled off by Indian raiders of no known tribe, whose only material needs appear to be spades and picks. Men who have spent a lifetime alone in the mountains are coming to town, not to celebrate the big strike, but to use their newly-broken fingers to sign away deeds to claims that then (alas, too late!) yield the riches they have dreamed of all their lives.

Make no mistake: silver mines, if they are to be productive and profitable, require men and resources. They are labor-intensive and require substantial financial investment. Some may see the future of Silvercliff in the advent of big business moving in. The corporation takes up where the individual makes a way for it. Is corporate citizenship a tenable concept? Perhaps so, but not as it has heretofore been practiced by the Silvercliff Mining Company, a company whose perfidy is apparent even in the name itself. Unless there really is a Silvercliff somewhere in Delaware.

# # #

*From the *Silvercliff Bugle,* June 19, 1882

The Bugle is alarmed to report further travesties perpetrated in violation of the laws of God and Man by the rascal Chicken Smith. His latest crimes occurred this Friday past, when, in broad daylight he robbed the Silvercliff Savings and Loan, overstuffed as it was that day with the Silvercliff Mining Company payroll and the fair-gotten gains of the bank's many depositors, most of whom are known to be the leading lights of this same company. It should come as a surprise to no one that the bank president, John "Crying Jack" Stanton, is closely associated with the man charged with leading the investigation, none other than our very own Sheriff Townes Marshall. We belabor these points only to remark on the amazing coincidences involved in Smith's choice of venue and the zealousness of law enforcement in attempting to apprehend the shameless villain.

It is a remarkable fact that, given the number

of witnesses in the bank who can attest to the events, no one seems to have noticed Smith's arrival in town. Those of a suspicious and cynical turn of mind might well suspect a certain factionalism in our fair city, allegiances divided along lines of attitude, toward order on the one hand, and lawlessness on the other. Apparently, the rule of law does not hold sway over a vast segment of our population, and would presumably include all the free citizens of Silvercliff about on the streets that day who did not raise the alarm at the approach of the nefarious Chicken Smith.

Be that as it may, the sheer bravado, bordering on foolhardiness, exhibited by Smith allowed him to get the drop on his victims. He quickly relieved the vault of valuables and would have left without incident were it not for the interference of Clem Wiggins, who was recently seen socializing with Sheriff Marshall as the latter was making his normal weekly collections. It is presumed that a large chunk of the cash which Smith was removing from the premises belonged to Wiggins, for he chose this most inopportune of moments to remark on Smith's unnatural fondness for domestic goats. With a wit that is quickly becoming proverbial, Smith inquired of Wiggins why he should so roundly condemn a practice observed regularly, and with tremendous gusto, by Wiggins' own father, whoever he might turn out to be. Taking a level of offense that was certainly understandable, if not exactly advisable, Wiggins attempted to draw the Derringer he customarily carried in his cummerbund. His weapon, however, never cleared his belt, for Smith's gun by then had executed summary judgment on two of Wiggins' fingers. The crack of a pistol and the sight of blood sent the masses fleeing in panic, leaving Smith free to spirit away some $15,000, and leaving Wiggins alone to await the ministrations of Dr. Stallings. The Bugle has been informed that Mr. Wiggins is expected to pull through with his own health and that of his remaining eight digits intact.

# # #

Letter, Abigail McSweeney to her sister, Alice, Oct. 17, 1876

Dear Alice,

I just wished to write you a short note to let you know that, after much aggravation and consternation, our home for foundlings, something of an orphan itself these past weeks, has found what we hope is a permanent address. It has been donated to us, free from encumbrances, by Cornelius Stark, a local merchant. The building, formerly used as a barn, but abandoned as the town encroached upon it, is in need of a great many repairs and alterations. However, we have found no shortage of volunteers here to assist in our endeavors. Indeed, the good people of Bentshaft have extended welcome and aid over and above what could reasonably be wished. Perhaps they endeavor to rescue the town's reputation from the serpents recently departed from their garden. How revolting you would have found them! Chief among their number was one John Stanton. The day the constables arrived to remove us from the property, there he was, in hat and tails, as if painting an outhouse changes the stench within! He affected to weep as children from two to twelve were turned out into the street! Snickering bystanders began calling him "Crying Jack." Apparently his cohorts found this amusing, and the name has stuck. These men have thankfully moved on, no doubt finding greener pastures to defile, and under the guise of legal financial institutions, making loans on impossible terms to the guileless, such as myself, foreclosing on desirable properties at their earliest convenience.

At any rate, I do not wish to make of this letter an undiluted stream of vitriol. It is, in fact, apparent that our temporary discomfort was part of the Almighty's greater design for a more enduring happiness. The children are busy learning to take pride and joy in the work of making a home, and while there was a bitter lesson to be learned concerning the avarice of men, there is the equally important knowledge gained of their essential good.

# # #

*From the *Silvercliff Bugle,* June 21, 1882

The citizens of Silvercliff have become accustomed to the almost impossible pace at which local outlaw Chicken Smith has managed to perpetrate his crimes. It is difficult to rouse our wonder anymore. However, the events of last Friday have given even the most jaded among us pause. Apparently, the brazen daylight robbery of the Silvercliff Savings and Loan, resulting in the near-death of the esteemed Mr. Clem Wiggins, was not enough to satisfy the blood-lust of the dastardly Smith. Smith, along with three masked accomplices, robbed the passengers of the Briggs-Parsons stage coach near Standish Wells, killing the driver and guard in the process.

What makes this deadly spree worthy of note is that witnesses put Smith in the Silvercliff bank at noon, while one of the stage coach passengers who managed to keep his pocket watch reports the hold-up occurred at approximately 12:30. That Chicken Smith managed to commit both these cowardly acts is indeed a fact to marvel at, especially given that Standish Wells is at least a two hour ride from Silvercliff. Apparently, not content to flout the laws of the land, Chicken Smith now dares to defy the laws set forth by that great legislator, Dr. Newton himself.

# # #

*Reward Notice, posted June 1882

PROCLAMATION
OF THE
SHERIFF OF GRANT COUNTY, ARIZONA
REWARD
FOR THE ARREST OF STAGE COACH ROBBERS

$100 for the delivery of Chicken Smith, $50 for information leading to the arrest of each of three unknown co-conspirators in the June 16 robbery of the Briggs-Parsons stage coach and the two killings attaching thereto.
    Sheriff Townes Marshall

# # #

*From the *Silvercliff Bugle,* Oct. 8, 1883

We are sad to report that another casualty can be put to the bloody account of Chicken Smith. That the incident involved a member of local law enforcement on an otherwise peaceful Sunday morning makes it all the more tragic.

Many of our readers are no doubt familiar with the victim, Deputy Sheriff Tiberius Lee, a stalwart officer who specializes in the art of forcible evictions, the legality of which might trouble the conscience of those without Lee's high convictions and low thoughtfulness. Apparently Deputy Lee's residence, far out of town and somewhat isolated, presented Chicken Smith with an opportunity he could not resist.

Testimony concerning the incident comes by way of Deputy Lee himself and one Jesus Garcia, a boy tending some cattle on the nearby ranch of James Solomon. Both Lee and Garcia were alerted to Smith's presence by the alarm sounded in the yard by Lee's poultry, several of which seem to have made their way into Smith's saddlebags. Apparently roused from slumber, Lee appeared on the porch, unsteady on his feet, according to Garcia, as if still half-asleep, or what is more likely, half-drunk, brandishing a shotgun. He discharged his weapon in the general direction of Smith and, in a statement provided by Garcia but not corroborated by Lee, managed to blast a good portion of his remaining poultry to bits.

What happened next is open to conjecture, since the statements of Lee and Garcia would seem beyond reconciliation. According to Lee, he stepped off his porch and prepared to fire again. Before he could do so, Chicken Smith fled on horseback, firing his pistol over his shoulder as he made his escape at a gallop, striking Lee in the foot and killing several more birds. While not as close to the action as Lee, we nonetheless print here the account provided by Garcia, for what it is worth. According to the young man, as soon as Lee fired his first shot, Smith was back in the saddle and in full retreat, firing a few stray shots behind him as cover. Lee stepped off his front porch, appeared to trip over his own feet, and in falling into his front yard accidentally discharged the shotgun, wounding himself in the foot and further depleting the local poultry population in a cloud of blood and feathers. While Deputy Lee is a sworn officer of the Court whose word is therefore beyond reproach, the fact that Dr. Stallings has stated that he removed only buckshot from the now three-toed left foot of the deputy would seem, at first blush, to lend credence to the story of Garcia. It does seem passing strange that buckshot should emerge from the muzzle of a Colt .45, though we do speak here of the Miracle Pistol of Chicken Smith.

# # #

*From *The Blazing Guns of Chicken Smith,* by Garrett Hartley

The coward Lee stood in his yard, shotgun held in his trembling hands, tremors of fear coursing through his craven limbs. With a dismissive scoff Smith turned away and mounted his horse.

"I shant do you as you deserve," Smith said as he spurred his steed back toward the hills and home. In his horse's polished silver bridle Smith could see Lee start to raise his gun.

"Hee-yah!" Smith shouted, and spurred his mount. As he galloped away, Chicken Smith drew his pistol and pointed it over his left shoulder. Sighting Lee's reflection once more in the shining bridle, Smith fired. The shotgun flew from the bloodied and astonished hands of Tiberius Lee.

"My own wickedness has done me in!" Lee exclaimed heavenward as he fell to his knees, clutching his bleeding and broken fingers to his breast. "Oh!, that I may live to repent my worthless life! Chicken Smith has spared me. May God bless him and have mercy on me!"

# # #

*From the *Silvercliff Bugle,* Nov. 20, 1883

We are elated to report that today the citizens of Silvercliff may breathe a collective sigh of relief and rest easy in their beds tonight; that incarnation of Crime itself has been apprehended. Chicken Smith sits in jail.

This most blessed event occurred late last night at Green's No. 6 Saloon, accomplished by Sheriff Townes Marshall and a group of four deputies. Acting upon a tip by an anonymous informant ("that drunken pigeon Waller" according to our own unnamed source) the Sheriff and his men entered the saloon just before midnight to find Chicken Smith seated at a table with three other upstanding Silvercliff citizens, engaged in the ancient art of seven card stud. Caught at last with his hands in the pot, Smith, without immediate recourse to his weapon, surrendered peacefully.

As of this writing, we are still eagerly anticipating the list of charges to be brought against Mr. Smith. If he is to be tried for all the crimes of which his is no doubt guilty, at least in the estimation of our most estimable sheriff, we may have to wait for quite some time for written documentation. We can only hope there is enough ink and paper in the territory to accomplish this task.

# # #

*From *Blood and Ink,* by Penwick Gathright

There was no doubt in my mind, or in the minds of Smith's many friends and sympathizers, that he could not possibly get a fair and impartial hearing in front of Judge Franklin Moorehouse. While it could be argued that since Smith was certainly guilty of robbing the savings and loan and the consequent wounding of Clem Wiggins, a lengthy prison term was justifiable, the powers that be would no doubt attempt to tack on as many peripheral incidents, real or imagined, as necessary in order to justify a punishment that would eventually end in a hanging. This type of "frontier justice" was all too common in Silvercliff at the time. The case of Gunther Bickerstaff comes to mind. He was an enterprising, if ornery man, who ran a small dry goods store. His was one of the first businesses in Silvercliff, and as such he served the needs of those early prospectors and entrepreneurs who embody for us now the spirit of the rugged pioneer carving out his place in the wilderness. Bickerstaff provided not only the material necessities for survival in early Silvercliff, but also by virtue of the fact that he owned a number of horses, mules, and wagons, he was instrumental in transporting goods and services and in maintaining connections and communications to outlying areas. As an individual operator serving the needs of other individual operators and smaller commercial mining outfits, he was thus a thorn in the side of the Silvercliff Mining Company in its bid at monopoly. Alas, the great strength of the rugged American pioneer is also his great weakness. The bold physicality which accounts for his tremendous capacity for hard work also explains the predilection for the corresponding level of rough play. The quick temper and decisive actions that equip him for survival in the mountains can have tragic consequences when deployed in town. Men such as Gunther Bickerstaff become the easily manipulated prey of slick operators such as the Silvercliff Mining Company. One evening, Bickerstaff committed the indiscretion of engaging in a public brawl of the drunken variety, during which it was alleged that he broke a man's jaw. That a dozen others were involved made not a whit of difference to Judge Moorehouse, who found Bickerstaff guilty of assault and battery. In imposing sentence, Moorehouse allowed a slew of hearsay testimony concerning Bickerstaff's character and behavior, including allegations of whoring and gambling, neither of which had the moral or legal implications they do today. Painted in the colors of every form of human depravity, Bickerstaff was condemned by Judge Moorehouse to serve fifteen years of hard time, while no one else involved in the altercation suffered any punishment worse than a night in jail and a five dollar fine.

Incidents such as these encouraged me to retain, on Smith's behalf, the services of Clifford Bunting, an old friend who was an accomplished attorney and former Territorial prosecutor. Among the many tactical blunders [Prosecutor Stephen] Enderby made in presenting his mountainous and ridiculous list of indictments against Smith, he chose to include the attempted murder of Tiberius Lee among them. By a nifty bit of legal maneuvering, Bunting was able to convince Moorehouse that since the Tiberius Lee incident occurred outside of Grant County proper, the correct venue for the trial would be the Federal courthouse in Cullahoolah. I have no illusions that had these arguments been put forth by someone of lesser stature than Clifford Bunting, Moorehouse would have simply dismissed them and moved ahead with the trial. However, as venal as Moorehouse was, even he knew that wrangling with Bunting would result in the unwanted involvement of Federal law enforcement, a level of authority which the Silvercliff Mining Company had not yet had the temerity to attempt to corrupt. As a further show of political clout, Bunting managed to have Smith removed from Sheriff Marshall's custody by none other than Federal Marshall Jake "Stand Alone" Allenby. With Smith's safety thus assured, I resolved to head to Cullahoolah to cover the trial.

# # #

From *The Encyclopedia of Shootists,* by Wes Carroll

By all accounts, few men in the annals of Western lore cut a more intimidating figure than Jake "Stand Alone" Allenby. He stood no less than six foot four and was described by Terry Fryman (*op cit*) as "a positive bear of a man." He apparently had a demeanor to match. He was known to be both fearless and relentless in the execution of his duties. He has been variously described as "stern," "upright," "pitiless," "inflexible," and "morally incorruptible."

More than once he was known to back down a lynch mob, risking his own life to ensure that a convicted criminal was afforded the proper execution promised him by law.

# # #

From *Showdown at Dawn,* by Clancy Yeager

Allenby earned the sobriquet "Stand Alone" in an episode reminiscent of the movie *High Noon.* In 1876, he was charged with transporting Hugh "Gullybunny" Blanton from jail in Tucson to stand trial in Sputtering Gulch, a two day ride. Blanton's gang made it known throughout the Territory that it was their intention that Blanton would never have to face a judge. While nothing ever came of these threats, the conspicuous absence of the public presence of any other members of the law enforcement community while Allenby and Blanton were abroad cemented Allenby's reputation as a larger than life defender of law and order. Following this, the mere rumor of Allenby's interest in a fugitive was known to effect surrender.

# # #

From the Silvercliff Bugle, Dec. 7, 1883

While we, as well as our attentive readers, have no doubt concerning the guilt that sits nightly upon the head of Chicken Smith, in the interest of fairness and journalistic integrity, the Bugle has obtained, and herein includes the substance of, an interview with the infamous Smith as he sat in the Cullahoolah jailhouse awaiting his trial on an as yet undisclosed number of charges; our able prosecutor Mr. Enderby, in consultation with other Grant County peace officers, as well as a committee of concerned local business men whose interests have been adversely effected by Smith's outrageous acts, are apparently busy burning the midnight oil, amending and adding charges in an effort to ensure public safety and that proper justice is done.

In all fairness, it must be said that in person Smith is not entirely without a certain charm. He is certainly no brute, grunting one word answers through the snarl of some untamed beast. Small in stature, though by no means frail, he is quick with a handshake and ready smile. Being caged and chained seems to have robbed him of neither his humor nor his self-possession. We spoke for perhaps an hour, during which time he made his justifications for his actions seem almost reasonable. Weaker minds might have been swayed from the fact that he is a dangerous criminal. Beware, dear reader, do not be persuaded by what may seem here to be soundest sense.

"On the advice of my attorney," he began, "I admit to nothing. The good people of Silvercliff know who I am and what I have done. And they also know why."

When asked who these "good people" were, Smith replied: "Folks in that town have worked hard to get what they have. Lord knows I am no choir boy, but I have never done any wrong to a man who makes an honest living. There is not a schoolteacher, pastor, widow, or orphan in that town who can say I have ever mistreated them. No store owner or bartender has ever stared into the barrel of my gun. Matter of fact, I never drew down on anyone who did not fire at me first, and everyone knows that. Everyone, even the crooked greasers who have turned me into the most wanted man in the Territory. Yes, even they know it."

When asked to expand on what might constitute a "crooked greaser," Smith had this to say: "Everyone in Silvercliff knows who I mean, though they might not say so out loud. There are the people who built the town and there are those who came in later, after the work was done, looking only to take what others worked so hard to make. We all know what no one can prove; that Sheriff Marshall and a few other local politicians and business men are the foot soldiers for Silvercliff Mining."

As anyone who reads the Bugle knows, we are certainly no friends of the Silvercliff Mining Company. It is with great discomfort that we find our own views on their activities to be aligned with those of a lawless heathen. However, unsettling though it may be, we must admit the fact that politics makes strange bedfellows, and on a few points we find ourselves in uneasy agreement with the opinions of an otherwise morally bankrupt soul. Whatever the merits of the case against Smith, his choice of victims would seem to speak volumes, if anyone in authority should care to learn the language.

# # #

*From KACS Radio Interview with Chester Gathright, March 1948

Question: Now, as I understand it, your grandfather never actually held public office, did he?
Chester Gathright: No, never, not that I'm aware of. I'm not sure whether or not he may have run for some

office at some point, but that was not really what he was interested in, that kind of direct power I mean. I think he was very concerned about the welfare of his community, about the quality of life in the town. He was very civic-minded, and very comfortable taking a public stance, but I think he felt that conventional politics was constraining. I mean, when you step into that arena, accepting a party platform, speaking to certain specific issues, there is a kind of, oh, compromise, I suppose, that he was not entirely comfortable with.

Q: But he did hold himself in opposition to an established political machine, did he not? The mining companies and so forth?

CG: Well, yes, he did. But here again, I think it is misleading to make it a simple black and white issue. It's easy to say that the Silvercliff Mining Company was in cahoots with certain representatives of the law, such as the sheriff and some judges. True enough. On the other side, you have what they would characterize as the lawless class, and this would include any kind of independent operator, prospectors whose imperfect understanding of the system might leave them open to accusations of squatting, loitering, claim-jumping.

Q: And Chicken Smith would have been included in the lawless class?

CG: Oh, certainly. But then again, people like my grandfather would have seen things differently. And we are not talking just about the lower classes of society here. Outside the county, at the federal level, you would have had U.S. marshals, federal judges, prosecutors, territorial authorities of all kinds who, at one time or another, might be more sympathetic to my grandfather's interests than those of Silvercliff Mining.

Q: So authority at the federal level was beyond

the reach of corruption by Silvercliff Mining?

CG: Look, no one here is naive enough to believe that the federal government, as embodied in the Territorial governing powers, was beyond being bribed or bought. But power at that level is a terribly complicated business, and you don't go stomping into it like a bull in a china shop. Silvercliff Mining was going to have to tread lightly in order to derive long-term benefits in the region. And the sad fact is, they had no intention of remaining in the region any longer than necessary.

Q: So in other words, could we say that it was, what?, more cost effective to come in and put your efforts into grabbing power at the local level?

CG: Exactly. Of course, when it came time to get Chicken Smith out of their reach, that turned out to be a tremendous advantage for him and my grandfather. And over time, it kept the fight at a manageable size. And in the end, of course, Silvercliff Mining packed up their tent in the middle of the night and left town.

Q: And any idea what became of them after that?

CG: Well, as I understand it, the company dissolved soon after. A few months later, an outfit called the Ambuscado Metals Exchange showed up in a Colorado boomtown, and from what I hear, a lot of the company officers had names that would have been familiar to folks in Silvercliff.

# # #

*From *Blood and Ink,* by Penwick Gathright

My initial salvo against the corrupt politicians and business men was met with what could be called clandestine intimidation. It was not unusual for me to arrive at my office in the morning and have my first task be sweeping up the glass from my front window that had been broken out during the night with a rock. Often the offending stone would have a note attached, warning me of my impending doom if I were to continue the course of my actions. A great many of the epistles on missiles were sent flying in the night in response to stories which the sender felt were biased in support of Chicken Smith at the expense of the good reputation of our stalwart sheriff, Mr. Townes Marshall. It has never been made clear to me to what extent I was meant to be fooled by the intentionally bad grammar and wretched spelling, or how gullible I was supposed to have been that I might believe that these acts of vandalism were being perpetrated by some of the good people of Silvercliff who were just trying to correct my erroneous support of the godless criminal Chicken Smith, while I unjustly undermined the authority of law enforcement.

# # #

*Letter, Chester Gathright to Wes Carroll, Jan. 19, 1974

Dear Mr. Carroll,

You recently wrote to me asking if I could share any recollections I may have concerning the outlaw Chicken Smith. As I am sure your research thus far has shown, I was not born until 1902, long after Smith had quit Silvercliff. When he returned in 1911, I knew him only as Barney Chantwell, a friend of my father's and grandfather's, who ran the Second Chance Saloon. It was several years before I was made aware of who he had once been. His identity was a family secret, at Chantwell's request, and he asked that it remain so until his death, after which I would be free to disclose any information I chose. To this day, I do not really know why he wished to avoid the issue, aside from the fact that he was, at this point in his life, a very private man. I suspect it also may have just been out of old habit, that my family had been colluding with him for so long that he simply wished to play the game out to the end. I think it was some strange kind of comfort to him that there was an elect that saw him truly, that if he hid himself from the majority of men, there would be those few out there who could, and would, set the record straight in the end. We were, and are, I suppose, the surprise character witnesses at his trial in the court of public opinion.

Of course, my grandfather's fondness for and defense of Chicken Smith are well attested. It is supposed by many that the connection between them was one of politics. At one end of the spectrum, are those who believed my grandfather used Smith as an unwitting pawn, while at the other end are those who saw them as co-conspirators in a grand and complex power play. Of course, neither of the extreme views is true. I believe my grandfather to have been a man who embraced his crusades as a public figure, who used his paper as a forum to assail the corruption he saw. I think Smith had common ground with him insofar as they both saw the same enemies—my grandfather saw them in the larger, public arena, Smith saw them in the smaller acts of certain individuals. Whatever Smith may have come to believe, I do not think he started out with well-considered political convictions, just his own sense of right and wrong. I do think he very quickly understood that my grandfather was fighting essentially the same battle, and that if he could be of use in furthering the cause, then so be it. I do not think it was any more complicated than that. In the years after he left Silvercliff, I think there were equal parts activist and trickster in his communications with my grandfather. I think he simply enjoyed rattling cages, and if Penwick Gathright benefited from that, so much the better. It seems to me that after a certain point, if Silvercliff benefited as well, then better yet. I cannot say when Chicken Smith, outlaw, became Barney Chantwell, citizen concerned with the welfare of Silvercliff, but somewhere between 1880 and 1900 he did. Of the intervening years, where he was and what he was doing, why he did not return to a place he clearly loved even after any enemies he may have had there were long gone, I cannot say. He never spoke of it, and I would never ask. While I would not describe him as secretive, I would say that he was not very forthcoming concerning his past, and while I would not describe him as intimidating, I would say there was something about him which was unapproachable.

All politics aside, there is a much simpler explanation for the bond between Pen Gathright and Chicken Smith, and it is something which is never mentioned in my grandfather's memoirs, with which you are obviously familiar, and which, of course, have been the basis for all the speculation regarding their relationship. The simple fact of the matter is that Chicken Smith risked his own life to save that of Penwick Gathright's son, my father Granville. It was in July of 1882. It was, as I'm sure you can well imagine, hot and dry. My father, then nine years old, was playing with some other boys in an old blacksmith's shop, abandoned for a year or more, and a regular, though disapproved of by parents, place for boys to gather and hatch their plots. Somehow, someone started a fire. As is often the case, the various accounts given by the boys would never add up to a coherent story. Whatever the case may be, conditions led to the fire quickly consuming the entire structure. My father, who had gone up into a small attic space, was trapped. The other boys fled the shack and raised the alarm. Unfortunately, the shack was at the very edge of the least populated part of town. No one would be able to arrive in time to rescue poor Granville. However, as Fate, Luck, or Providence would have it, Chicken Smith was in the vicinity and saw what was happening. I cannot answer with any certainty why he was nearby, though as I say this end of town was sparsely populated. Smith was no stranger to Silvercliff at the time, and when about his furtive business in town, this is likely the area he would have been based in. Whatever the case may be, Smith rode up to the shack, grabbed his bedroll from behind his saddle, and stood on the back of his horse to gain access to a small vent in the attic. He apparently had no trouble busting out enough boards to get in—he was, remember, fairly slight of build. He grabbed my father, wrapped him in the blanket, and headed for the exit. Smith lowered my father as far as he could, then dropped him down onto his horse. It was at that moment the building collapsed. The horse bolted out of the way as Smith came crashing down, rolling away as the shack fell down in flames around him. A piece of burning wood struck him on his left arm as he raised it to protect his head, causing the scar by which we always knew him afterward. He was not injured extensively, and only my father, grandfather, and Dr. Clement Stallings knew it was there. It never became a feature by which he could be identified except by those privy to it. When Barney Chantwell came to Silvercliff in 1911, almost thirty years older, that mark was still there to vouchsafe his identity. Whatever philosophical, political, or ethical similarities or differences they could have had, this one incident would have secured my grandfather's loyalty. Historians today seem to wish to see large, impersonal forces at work in the events of the past in order to justify some theory of economics or sociology. Sometimes the genesis of the momentous is as simple as the kindness that one man does another.

I hope this material has been of help to you. Feel free to contact me if you have any further questions. Sincerely,
Chester Gathright

# # #

*Cullahoolah Daily Register, Dec. 10, 1883

DARING JAILBREAK!
OUTLAW CHICKEN SMITH FLIES COOP!
DESPERADO STILL AT LARGE!

At approximately 12:45 yesterday afternoon, a daring escape was made from the local lock-up by noted badman Chicken Smith. Smith, who was awaiting trial on a number of serious charges, including armed robbery and attempted murder, took advantage of a lapse in attentiveness by the local constabulary during meal time and slipped out of his cell on the jail's second floor. A lithe and nimble spirit indeed, Smith went out a window and, with the agility and surefootedness of a mountain goat, utilized niches in the building's masonry and some obliging tree branches to swiftly gain the ground. He absconded with a horse that was hitched nearby and, with most of the locals taking advantage of their day of rest, few people were about that could have helped mount effective pursuit. At the time this paper went to press, Smith was still at large. He is rightly considered armed and dangerous.

# # #

*The *Silvercliff Weekly Trumpet,* Dec. 14, 1883

News Worthy of Note: We can't help but wonder at the good fortune of Chicken Smith. Are we alone in finding it suspicious that a horse, freshly saddled and roaring to go, was just sitting there, like it was waiting for him? We here at the Trumpet know the foul doings of that most respectable of criminals, Penwick Gathright, when we see it. We sure hope Mr. Gathright's comeuppance is swift and sure, what with his endless attempts, using the guise of a respected member of the Fourth Estate, to corrupt and upset the fine city we have founded out here midst the sage brush and silver-coated hills.

He is dissolved once again into the landscape. He passes among his fellow men like blown dust or unremarked tumbleweeds. No one pays heed to the shimmering heat warping the horizon, no one notices the lull in a cricket's song at the approach of Chicken Smith.

He is no ghost, for he haunts not; he is no shadow, for he moves in darkness; he is no legend, for his bones wear flesh.

#

Silvercliff Bugle, Letter to the Editor, February 17, 1885

Dear Sirs:

I feel it is my duty, as the counterpart to the law abiding citizens of Silvercliff, to let them know that the tax dollars, bribes, hush money, and extortions to which they are routinely subject are being put to good use. Even at the remote outpost of San Francisco, California, the reach of that great peace officer, and yes I mean you Sheriff Townes Marshall, can be felt. I fear daily for my freedom, indeed my very life. In fact, I think I can safely say that I expect capture here just as likely as I ever did back in Silvercliff. The Lion of Silvercliff got lucky once; who's to say lightning may not strike the same man twice in a lifetime? I only hope the voters of Grant County allow him the lifelong appointment he will need in order to effect his high moral purposes. From what I hear, the base of his support is being diluted daily by those ruffians and hooligans who wish to plunge the Territory back into the Dark Ages, when a man worked his own claim and ploughed his own field. If these so-called reformers succeed, what will become of all the poor stuffed vests sitting on the board of Silvercliff Mining? Damn the re-platting proposal sponsored by Mr. Gathright and Maj. Hornsby. Or perhaps it is too late. Unless, of course, the good Sheriff could bring off a real political coup, maybe bring in the most

wanted man in the county? Mr. Marshall, here I am. Come and get me.
Sincerely yours,
Chicken Smith

# # #

Silvercliff Bugle, Letter to the Editor, Jan. 4, 1899

Dear Sirs:

Greetings from the revivifying springs of Las Vegas, New Mexico. As a man of infamy and bad reputation, I come here following in the footsteps of my spiritual ancestors and brethren, to whit: the likes of Rattlesnake Sam, Hook Nose Jim, Stuttering Tom, Cock-Eyed Frank, and a host of other outlaw worthies. They say that some years back, Billy the Kid's pickled finger showed up here. Perhaps some day the same will become of my nose, which Mr. Townes Marshall would no doubt like to cut off to spite my face. If not, perhaps, his own. Or is it not true as I have heard that he has been divested of that authority? Seems almost coincidental that the legal land holdings of the Silvercliff Mining Company have been similarly shorn of grandeur in recent years, reduced to a more modest and democratically spirited size. In all honesty, I do congratulate the people of Silvercliff, including yourself, Mr. Gathright, who have fought the good fight and finally succeeded in curbing the land- and money-lust of a host of rapacious foes. As always, I remain duly impressed,
Chicken Smith
P.S. The sunset awaits. Perhaps it is time I rode off toward it.

# # #

*From *Blood and Ink,* by Penwick
Gathright

Perhaps I should not admit this, having spent a good
portion of my life attempting to champion the truth,
but when it came to the facts of the career of Chicken
Smith, I was not always the most conscientious
fact-checker, nor can I pretend that my journalistic
instincts always steered me on an objective course.

# # #

St. Louis Post-Gazette, Jan. 23,
1899

Penelope Chantwell, age 62, passed away yesterday.
She is survived by her sister, Camellia Roberts, and
son Barnabus. Services to be held Saturday, 11 a.m.,
at Blanford Funeral Home, after which she will be
laid to rest in Franklin's Field Cemetery, beside her
beloved daughter Collette.

The mention of Barnabus in Penelope
Chantwell's obituary leads me to
believe that mother and son remained
in contact over the years, though no
documentary evidence has been found
to support this claim, and there is
nothing to indicate that Barnabus
Chantwell ever returned to St. Louis
after 1873. However, the fact that he
is mentioned as surviving her is a
clear indication that the family knew

he was still alive at the very least, and it strongly implies that all parties involved were not estranged. Finally, the following passage in *Mary Tucker, *Poems,* is marked and dated Feb. 19, 1899:

> I am weary, Mother, and I fain would rest
> Beside thee, in the cold and silent tomb—
> ("I Am Weary, Mother" p. 14)

Again, while no evidence has been found that Chantwell visited St. Louis after leaving at the age of thirteen, there is the intriguing possibility that he may have done so upon his mother's death. The last letter from Chicken Smith to the *Silvercliff Bugle* is dated Jan. 4, 1899, sent from Las Vegas, NM. It is possible that the death of his mother, along with rekindled memories of his beloved sister, resulted in another fundamental change in his way of life comparable to that occasioned by Collette's death in 1873. At any rate, "Chicken Smith" disappears from the historical record, never to return. Barnabus Chantwell remains missing until 1911.

He stands alone in the mist drifting riverward from the newer grave. His head so seldom bare, his thinning hair protests each gust of wind. Barnabus once more for the moment, he wipes the moisture from his face; tears or rain, there's none to say. Certain years have been bracketed closed. Words, as words often do, have failed him, and the rest, sayeth the Bard, is silence. He walks away, toward the missing horizon where the dawn should be.

# # #

It has long been supposed that "Chicken Smith" was not the only alias used by Barnabus Chantwell, and that this would help account for the long periods during which he makes his presence known to his allies in Silvercliff from a specific place without anyone there recalling his presence (1884-1899), or during which he disappears from the public record entirely (1899-1911). The following tantalizing documents were found among the Gathright papers, and though none can be definitively proven to have been written by Chantwell, the style, subject matter, and other internal evidence would appear to make the case nearly certain. They are written in what appears to be a disguised hand, most likely by the right-handed Chantwell using his left hand. The most important point is that though several different names, all obviously whimsical, are used, all these letters are unquestionably written by the same person. Thus, if any one of them can be shown to have been written by Barnabus Chantwell, then all of them were.

Letter to Penwick Gathright, dated Aug. 28, 1902

Dear Mr. Gathright,

I understand congratulations are in order. It seems you have survived a most violent time in our nation's history, as well as all the flux and danger of your own locale, long enough to become a grandparent. Give your son and his lovely wife my best. May young Chester continue the family tradition of shaping the world around him into a place of honesty and decency. May he avoid a condition I find all too common among the educated young in the northeast of these United States. I am sure it would come as a shock to many that money and privilege are no guarantee of common sense. I truly fear for the future of our great nation if some of these young men manage to buy their way into power and thereby determine our economic and political future. But I digress.

I chanced to meet a young man (I forget his name, Frank something-or-other; I shall remember it shortly), the editor-in-chief of the Harvard Daily Crimson. He seemed remarkable at first only in being a Democrat, but I quickly noticed that he had a fine mind and a somewhat skeptical streak toward the value of what he was being taught. He is certainly ambitious, and a young man possessed of political convictions to such a degree that he is actively engaged in supporting Bryant's campaign, even though Mr. Roosevelt is not only an avowed hero, but

a distant relative as well. At any rate, as we spoke, he made some comment, the content of which I don't remember, but it concerned something he spoke of as making him fearful. Quite casually, I said, "Well you know what Thoreau said—'nothing is so much to be feared as fear.'" "That's good," he said, quickly grabbing pen and paper, "I have to remember that one." And in my mind, he will no doubt make use of it in the future. Such are the minor satisfactions of dealing with the youth of today. At any rate, until we meet again, I remain
Sincerely yours,
Crispin Farquar

Letter to Granville Gathright, Oct. 17, 1903. Though this letter begins as if it is being submitted to the editor of the *Silvercliff Bugle,* a title which Granville had assumed from his father earlier in the year, it was not published. In addition, it appears that it was sent to Gathright's home address and not that of the newspaper, since it was found with other personal correspondence in the collection of Gathright's papers. It would appear this letter, if written by the legendary Chicken Smith, is a bit of sly comic playfulness, gently poking fun at the myth of the Old West.

Dear Mr. Gathright,

I thought your readers might find it of interest that in my brief visit to the justly fabled city of New

York, I managed to come face to face with a true legend of the West, and newspaper man like yourself, the renowned Bat Masterson.

I met him one afternoon in a saloon frequented by the city's sporting class. I must say, in person and at first glance, one would never guess this to be the man responsible, as every educated person is well aware, for the deaths of over two dozen men during gunplay on the dusty streets of towns all across the West. He appears no more larger than life than you or I. But as we all know, first impressions can be deceptive. Solidly built and outgoing, he is the center of attention of the group he is in, a certain self-possession and confidence inspiring respect from those in his company.

As the day wore on and evening fell, I found myself seated for a short spell at a table alone with Mr. Masterson. While I am no legend myself, I found over the course of our conversation that we had many things, persons, places, experiences, in common. It seems our paths across the West had criss-crossed several times, and at least once we had apparently found ourselves at the same place at the same time: the title fight between Jim Corbett and Robert Fitzsimmons, in Carson City, back in 1897. It is well-known around town that Masterson is an avid scholar of the sweet science, and though I am far from expert in such matters, I did have a certain appreciation for the principals in this particular bout. As far as heavyweights go, both men were of smallish size. As a gent on the slight side myself, I admired their ability to thrive against the big boys. Both were excellent technicians, Fitzsimmons using his wonderful sense of leverage and space to generate tremendous punching power, Corbett using quickness, of both mind and body, to anticipate and counter the more brutish attacks employed by most fighters.

This is just one example of our shared interests. As Mr. Masterson warmed to the whiskey and conversation, we spoke of things more personal, intimate. As we talked privately, he became more reflective, and displayed a kind of humility I did not expect. He dispensed with playing up to his image with me, as if he felt I could have seen through any pretensions he may have attempted. Perhaps I, or more accurately the drink, said something that gave him the impression we were somehow equals, that I could understand the perils and pressures of his kind of fame, though I can't imagine what that would have been. I would never presume to compare my own meager accomplishments with those of the Gun Who Won the West. But whatever the events that brought about this confluence, as we staggered out into the bright Broadway night and made our effusive farewells, I found myself most glad that I had the opportunity to speak with a living legend.
Sincerely,
Salvator Q. Pickering

Letter to Penwick Gathright, Sept. 27, 1905

Dear Penwick,

I hope this letter finds you in fine health and enjoying the fruits of a well-earned retirement. Time, my old friend, does not seem to pass by, so much as gain momentum with each passing year. Such ruminations found themselves recently picked up and considered by what most would think of as a chance encounter. Time, coincidence, fate, free will:

the stuff of philosophy and, it would appear, modern physics. Can it be considered chance that even as I am contemplating the nature of time I would run into a young man who is even now on the brink of discoveries that are sure to shake our view of the world to its very foundations? Well, perhaps not our world. That is the hazard of aging. The world opens anew for each generation of young geniuses. Newton defined the world in which we have lived; perhaps this lad will become a similar founder for his. If you think I exaggerate, you might be correct. What do I know of such lofty subjects?

My recent tour brought me to the lovely city of Bern as I was traveling from Geneva to Zurich. I had lunch one day at a cafe that catered to what we might call the 'working-man', including a clerk in the patent office. His name was Albert, and we began a conversation over after meal drinks. Several in fact. What struck me most about him was that, scientist though he is, he appears more mystic than mechanistic. He has apparently already made quite a name for himself based on the papers he has already published this year, and now has another going to press as we speak that he assures me will revolutionize our entire concept of reality. Between my lack of training in the subject and the action of the wickedly delicious local beer, I could scarce keep up with him. His math, scrawled on a damp napkin, looked simple enough, but he flatly states that the implications are of cosmic proportions, literally. It seems he has proposed and proven nothing less than the equivalence of matter and energy. (!!!) I could think of nothing to say in the face of such bizarre and, to my mind, illogical notions, except to quote my old second in any mental duel, Emerson: "Nature's dice are always loaded."

To which my young friend replied in all earnestness: "Mein Gott doss not play viss deisse." All in all, by far my most stimulating, if confounding, conversation since I landed on the Continent. Who knows what novel concepts I may stumble upon as I go farther afield in the Old World.

Sincerely,

Col. Eustace Specklewood

Whither Smith now in his confusion of names? None can say, his pathways traceable only in isolated letters, the fossil poetry by which we reconstruct him.

# # #

*From the Silvercliff Bugle, Sept. 18, 1911

While it may pass the notice of the younger generation, there was a ripple of nostalgia among the old-timers today as the Second Chance Saloon opened its doors for business. Some few readers may recognize the location as the building which once housed the most notorious den of iniquity in old Silvercliff, the Rusty Pick Saloon. New proprietor Barnabus Chantwell recently moved to our fair berg from parts unknown, bringing with him his lovely bride of six months and enough ready cash to purchase and refurbish the abandoned old building on what has become a side of town less frequented by the majority of law-abiding citizens. Mr. Chantwell tells us that it is his hope that his will merely be the first of several new businesses in the area, with the intention of returning to that end of town some of the luster that it once had. We wish him well in this endeavor, and intend to show our support and unofficial endorsement by partaking in refreshments there later this evening.

# # #

*Tawaka County Clerk Records, County Courthouse, Cullahoolah, AZ, dated March 4, 1911

Entered into matrimony on this day, Barnabus Chantwell, Silvercliff, AZ; and Marisol Castillo, Texas—ceremony performed by Judge Carson Cavanaugh, Tater Collins standing as witness thereof.

# # #

*From the *Silvercliff Bugle,* Dec. 23, 1913

It is with great sadness that we report the passing yesterday of Marisol Chantwell while giving birth to a stillborn baby boy. Mrs. Chantwell is survived by her husband Barnabus, the proprietor of the Second Chance Saloon.

According to Mr. Chantwell, his wife was born Marisol Castillo, in northern Mexico in 1887. Her father was Capt. Manuel Castillo of the Mexican army. Her mother, known to us only as Pilar, had been captured as a small child by a band of Apaches and raised as one of their own. She was apparently rescued as a teenager, at which time she is presumed to have met Capt. Castillo. Nothing more of her fate is known. Marisol's father was apparently killed in a skirmish with bandits while she was still an infant, whereupon she was taken in and raised in a convent on the Texas side of the border. It was here that, about three years ago according to Mr. Chantwell, they met. He states that he had spent a good part of his life traveling extensively and was now ready to settle down, and that for her part, she was desirous of leaving the convent. They were married at the court house in Cullahoolah, for sentimental reasons according to Mr. Chantwell, in March of 1911, after which they settled in Silvercliff.

# # #

*From the *Silvercliff Bugle,* Feb. 15, 1912

On what had to be one of the most festive Wednesdays in the annals of modern Silvercliff, several thousand people gathered to celebrate Arizona's newfound membership in the United States of America. Grant Park was the scene, and what a scene it turned out to be. Music was provided throughout the day by such local luminaries as Chigger Watson and the Slow-Drip Boys, Fat Fred Thompson and his Cowboy Clan, and the always entertaining minstrelsy of Croonin' Clark Kennedy. A host of Silvercliff's finest eateries and drinkeries provided refreshments, with the always popular smoked whole hogs of Chantwell's Second Chance Saloon leading the way. The evening's fireworks display resulted in far fewer injuries than anticipated by the Fire Department, so it is generally accepted that the entire affair was a complete success.

# # #

*From the *Silvercliff Bugle,* Oct. 19, 1919

It is with heavy heart and a deep sense of personal loss that we note the passing yesterday of Penwick Garthright at the age of 73. He is survived by his wife of 48 years, Kathleen, their son Granville, and grandson Chester.

Penwick Gathright was a resident of Silvercliff almost from the time of the town's founding in 1878. With the town's tremendous early growth, Mr. Gathright saw the need for a community organ through which the burgeoning populace could sort out the oftentimes confusing news of the day. Thus, in 1879 the *Silvercliff Bugle* was born. Not content merely to chronicle the who, what, and where of events, Penwick Gathright was determined to delve into the why as well. This led him inevitably into the role of not only a recorder of history, but also its shaper. The story of present day Silvercliff is impossible to tell without recounting that of Penwick Gathright as well. He remained at the helm of the *Bugle,* through times both good and bad, secure as well as perilous, until his retirement in 1903, at which time the present editor, his son Granville, took over leadership of the paper. To say that Penwick Gathright will be missed is both an understatement and a gross falsehood. His spirit is present and in evidence everywhere throughout Silvercliff. Anyone walking along Main Street, enjoying the tree-lined avenue amidst the bustle of the thriving businesses, past the public parks resounding with the shouts of play, and into the warmth and safety of his home, walks with Penwick Gathright at his side.

# # #

*From the *Silvercliff Bugle,* July 23, 1938.

For one evening, at the Second Chance Saloon last night, the Wild West returned to Silvercliff. Though the Second Chance is normally a venue where fellowship, good cheer, and a (sometimes boisterous) civility are to be found, even the friendliest atmosphere, under the influence of alcohol, heat, and a payday crowd, can turn menacing. Such was the case last night, when an altercation arose between patrons Stanley Thursby and Benny Compton. While we know little of Stanley Thursby's character, Mr. Compton's name will be familiar to those readers who routinely peruse the police blotter. He has been arrested several times for drunk and disorderly conduct and has spent some time in the local lock-up for assault and battery. By all accounts, it was he who initiated the action, though the point of dispute between the two men remains unknown to us at this time.

According to witnesses, Mr. Compton was obviously intoxicated. Mr. Abraham Vettner, who was there at the time and later gave a statement to the police, tells the *Bugle* that "it all happened kind of sudden like. That Compton fella, I guess he must have been pretty well oiled, but it wasn't like he was being loud and bothering people. Barney [Chantwell, proprietor of the Second Chance] wouldn't have put up with that. Anyway, Compton just starts in on the other guy Thursby, I don't know why. Next thing I know, out comes Compton's blade. I didn't see nothing up to then that could explain why he pulled a knife on the guy."

Jeremiah Barnes, who it seems was a bit closer to the action, said, "I don't know what the boys were discussing, but at some point it got a bit heated. Compton stood up and yelled a few choice words I ain't going to repeat here. He gave Thursby a little shove, and Thursby kind of backed away. He didn't seem to want a fight, but I think he might have muttered a little something under his breath that Compton took offense to. That was when Compton pulled out a knife and went for the guy."

What happened next was a marvel to even the most seasoned observers of Silvercliff's sometimes overly exuberant night life.

"It happened quick as that," stated Fidelio Ramirez, snapping his fingers. "Compton went for the guy with his knife, and all of a sudden, boom! Went deaf for a second, big puff of smoke. Then things got real quiet all of a sudden for a second. I turned around, and there's old Barney [Chantwell], standing behind the bar, calm as you please, Colt in one hand, dialing the phone with the other. I looked back over at Compton and he's on his knees, holding his bloody arm, knife just lying there on the floor. Nobody moved for a good long while."

All the other witnesses interviewed for this article concurred that the entire affair lasted only seconds, an end put to it by proprietor Barney Chantwell with a decisiveness and finality that still has the patrons of the Silver Strip buzzing.

# # #

From the journal of Granville Gathright, Oct. 3, 1927.

I had occasion today to stop in for lunch at the 2nd Chance. As always, a good crowd. As usual, Barney questioned my motives before taking me through to the back room. "Got to make sure you're not hiding a G-man under that jacket." A running joke.

Finally had a chance to sit and talk with Sylvia Diamond. Met her a few times briefly, but have never conversed in any depth. She and Barney have been keeping company almost since the day she got to town three years ago. She is as reticent as he is, but made the cryptic remark that she and Barney had known one another years ago, and that she once "helped him out of a jam." She is a mass of contradictions. Small, handsome, sixty-ish, unassuming in dress, quiet in demeanor. Yet something about her, the way she can hold her own in a room of carousing men, the sudden witticism as defensive maneuver, bespeaks a past that is not that of a school marm. Like Barney, she is friendly, but not forthcoming, and it is my suspicion that in all likelihood it is for similar reasons.

From the journal of Chester Gathright, Aug. 16, 1943

Went to visit Barney Chantwell today. Sylvia passed away yesterday. Twenty years together. Barney poured us each a brandy, and we raised a glass to her. There was something peaceful about him, sad but not grief-stricken. He seems a man no longer haunted by loss. He spoke of their shared life, at length but without being very specific. He had apparently somehow, somewhere known her before she came to Silvercliff. Not that surprising given Barney's years of restlessness. At any rate, it struck me that she had given him some sense of continuity in his life, a bridge that reached from Chicken Smith to Barney Chantwell. He referred to her at one point as a fallen angel who had regained a state of grace, and that this was something he could readily understand. Something also about the shared scars of their pasts. I assumed he was speaking figuratively, but when he spoke he made a curious gesture with his left arm that made me wonder. Barney remains as mysterious to me as ever.

These are the only two mentions of the woman with whom Chantwell apparently spent two decades of his life. The name "Sylvia Diamond" is almost certainly a pseudonym. It may have been a stage name (though no performer of that name appears in any documentary evidence, such as a handbill or newspaper advertisement), or the alias of a prostitute.

Old wounds heal, only the memory opening again upon reaquaintance. Scars fade as skin loosens above the shrinking flesh, though recollection remains as sharp as the original pain.

# # #

*From the diary of Emma Markson, Dec. 19, 1881

Much talk among the men folk in the parlor this evening. Seems two more local mining co's sold out today. I have no truck with politics, but I do admit to falling prey at times to the seductive powers of Rumor. I am not always sure to what degree Mr. Gathright's paper maintains its loyalty to the truth, but most of my acquaintances seem to sympathize with his attitude toward Silvercliff Mining. This evening's edition seems to have gotten everyone up in arms over the perceived depredations the aforementioned outfit committed in order to acquire the properties of the latest sellouts. The great counter-weight to the gravity of the situation would seem to be the Bugle's champion, the outlaw Smith. There is much rib-nudging and snickering at the expense of the Sheriff. I myself cannot say whether or not there is a case to be made concerning Smith's criminality, or the criminality of the Sheriff for that matter. I have never formally met either one. But there does seem to be a great deal of attention paid to this man Smith who is seldom present in town and who is, by all accounts of those persons whose opinions I respect, a decent and even honorable man. His only crimes would appear to be against the dignity of Mr. Marshall. Must remember to set aside one of my pies for Mrs. Beardsley; she has not felt terribly well since her son Mason enlisted.

# # #

*From *Blood and Ink,* by Penwick Gathright

Lest you, my reader, think me alone and eccentric in my estimation of [Chicken] Smith's character, allow me to quote a letter, printed in the *Bugle* in May of 1882, from one Marcus Freeman, a man with whom I was not at all acquainted at the time:

Dear Editor:

In response to the recent article your paper ran concerning the alleged crimes of Chicken Smith, I thought that perhaps someone with first-hand knowledge of the man should speak up, as I feel he is certainly getting a raw deal from the law. I thought at first the same could be said of this paper, but I understand now that you are only meaning to poke fun at Sheriff Marshall. I have never had any dealings with the man, but he must be very foolish indeed if he thinks he fools anyone with his false accusations against Smith. I have met Smith a couple of times in the course of my business, which often takes me out of town and into some fairly wild and dangerous places. I am not trying to make myself out to be a very brave man, as I am not. I only want people to know that under such conditions, if a man wishes you harm, and he is as accomplished a bad man as Smith is made out to be, well, best of luck to you, for you will need it. All that I mean to say is that I have crossed paths with Smith on two separate occasions in remote areas and me with enough ready cash and goods on my person that I might make a tempting target to a desperado. On the first occasion we met while riding in opposite directions on the trail that connects the Deercorn Lode and Wambaugh's Strike. I did not in fact know this was Chicken Smith at the time. He was just a young man on horseback, coming at a good pace away from the Deercorn. He slowed when he saw me, and asked if I was headed up to Deercorn to do some trading. I said I was. He said that I would indeed be in luck if I had any blasting powder for sale, for they were plum out. He winked at me and laughed, then spurred his horse away. Only later, after I learned who he was and that the Deercorn had just been bought out by

Silvercliff Mining did I have my suspicions about that missing powder. The other time we met was in an old miner's shack on Pokerface Ridge. A violent storm had come up, and I felt lucky to have come across this shelter. I walked in to find this same young man I had met once before, sitting before a fire he had started in a makeshift fireplace. He seemed to recognize me as well, and welcomed me in and offered me a cup of coffee. We talked for a bit and he told me who he was. I must have looked a bit startled, because he smiled and said not to worry none, he meant me no harm. In fact, he shared the meal he had prepared and the little whiskey that he had with him. He seemed on his guard at first, but after awhile he relaxed and we got on well enough. How he knew I would not betray him or his whereabouts I do not know. I suppose he saw I was no threat right then, and that by the time I could find the authorities he would be long gone anyway. So we passed a few pleasant hours, passing his flask back and forth and playing chess on a board I had for barter. I suppose I ramble on at length here just to show anyone out there on the fence about whether or not Smith is as deadly and desperate as some say, he is not. And I never met anyone who has actually met Chicken Smith who says different.

Regards,
Marcus Freeman

# # #

From a letter, Chicken Smith to Granville Gathright, Aug. 12, 1896

Dear Granville,

    I suppose part of the 'charm' as you put it of Silvercliff to me is the quality of the majority of the population. As Emerson said, God offers to every mind its choice between truth and repose. Take which you please—you cannot have both. It would have been easy for that majority, swayed by the promise of reward offered by wealthy and powerful men, to have given me up at most any time. But it seems to me that Silvercliff enjoys a preponderance of honorable men who choose Truth. Such society, rare at all times, but especially so in a mining boomtown where fortunes are made and lost overnight, should be cherished and encouraged. Whatever my faults, and they are no doubt numerous, I have always tried to make my missteps outside the law adversely affect only the fortunes of those who do not do right by the public good, at least as I interpret the phrase. The fact that your father, a man for whom I have the utmost respect and admiration, seems to interpret it as I do lends confidence to my beliefs...

This letter would seem to be a response to some kind of communication from Granville Gathright to Smith. What the form of that communication was we have no clues. There is no evidence that Smith had a fixed address at which he could have received written correspondence at this time. In fact, his letters of the time are sent from all over the United States. On the other hand, Granville Gathright's itinerary, which is easy enough to reconstruct, allows for the possibility of a face to face meeting. Where or when such a meeting might have taken place is entirely conjectural, however. Another, though less likely scenario, would be that Granvilles's remarks were conveyed to Smith by a third party, Penwick Gathright being the most obvious candidate. However, there is no evidence from Smith's letters or the known movements of Penwick Gathright that any meeting, of any kind, took place between the two during the period 1884-1911.

With the roar of blood not his alone in his ears, he was gone, a slight smile in his final moments the bequeathed token of a life well spent. With the barest recognizable flicker the Old West died, even as a new sun rose in the East, birthing in the shower of its radiation a New World, as vast and unexplored as, in its infancy, the Old One just eclipsed.

# # #

Epilogue

The following is the only bit of verse that can reliably be attributed to Barnabus Chantwell. It was found, handwritten on a scrap of unlined paper, sitting loose between two moleskin journals belonging to Granville Gathright. The last entry in one journal is dated June 1923, the first entry in the second one July 1923, confirming the sequence of the journals as found. However, there is nothing to indicate whether or not the poem was written during this period. It is untitled and unsigned, though analysis of the handwriting confirms it was written by Chantwell, but the date range, based on well-attested documents, can only be narrowed to the years between 1911 and 1931. Based on where it was found in the Gathright archives, 1923 seems as reasonable a date of composition as any. It should be noted that the poem as we have it is neatly printed, without correction or revision. This has led some scholars to believe that Chantwell had sent it to Gathright for possible publication, while others think that it was perhaps authored by someone else and Chantwell had copied it out for himself. Both proposals are purely speculative; however, it seems reasonable to suppose, barring evidence to the contrary, that the poem is Chantwell's original composition.

The air I breathe
'S been breathed before
By fine-haired gent
And Scragtown whore

I gave up searching
For places new
That I ain't seen
And neither have you

Once untamed West
Is now mildest East
The wild mountain cat
A domestic beast

So I come back here
To put down roots
My chosen homeland
Underneath my boots

The moon above's
The one I've always seen
The place I love's
Where I've always been

# # #

Appendix: Chronology

1837(?) Penelope Chantwell born.

1846 Penwick Gathright born.

1849 "Resistance to Civil Government" by Henry David Thoreau published in the anthology *Aesthetic Papers.*

1858 Collette Chantwell born.

1860 Barnabus Chantwell, alias Chicken Smith, born in St. Louis, MO.
     Ralph Waldo Emerson publishes *The Conduct of Life.*

1861(?) Death/disappearance of Spencer Chantwell.

1867 Jess Chisolm opens the trail named after him.

1871 Aug. 19, Newton Massacre

1873 Sept. 17, Granville Gathright born.
     Death of Collette Chantwell by drowning in Mississippi River, an apparent suicide.
     Barnabus Chantwell, alias Chicken Smith, leaves home.

1874 June 5, Second Battle of Adobe Walls.

1875 Feb. 27, letter from Penelope Chantwell to her son, confirming his presence at Throckmorton's Lazy J Ranch in Central Texas.

1876 Chantwell leaves Throckmorton, Ellsworth, KS.
     June 24, the St. Louis Brown Stockings defeat the Philadelphia Athletics, 8-3.
     June 25, Custer's Last Stand.

1878 Founding of Silvercliff, AZ following the discovery of large silver deposits in the nearby hills.

1879 Penwick Gathright begins publishing the *Silvercliff Bugle.*

1880 Barnabus Chantwell, alias Chicken Smith, arrives in Silvercliff, sometime in the spring.
    May 17, shootout between Chicken Smith and Calvin Jenkins.
    May 18, standoff at Brownwell's livery.

1882 June 17, holdup of Silvercliff Savings and Loan; Briggs-Parsons stage coach robbery.
    July, Chicken Smith rescues Granville Gathright.

1883 Oct. 7, shooting of Tiberius Lee.
    Nov. 19, arrest of Chicken Smith.
    Dec. 9, Cullahoolah jailbreak.

1887 Marisol Castillo born.

1889 *The Blazing Guns of Chicken Smith,* by Garrett Hartley, published.

1896 Granville Gathright on honeymoon in Naples, Italy.

1899 Jan. 22, death of Penelope Chantwell.

1901 Feb. 25, Joe Choynski defeats Jack Johnson (KO 3), in Galveston, TX.

1902 May 27, Chester Gathright born.

1903 Granville Gathright takes over as editor/publisher of the *Silvercliff Bugle.*

1905 The *annus mirabilis* of Albert Einstein.

1911 Mar. 4, Barnabus Chantwell, alias Chicken Smith, marries Marisol Castillo in Cullahoolah, AZ.
Barnabus Chantwell, alias Chicken Smith, returns to Silvercliff and opens the Second Chance Saloon.

1912 Feb. 14, Arizona is admitted to the Union, becoming the 48th state.
Carlisle wins the national collegiate football championship, led by Jim Thorpe's 25 touchdowns and 198 points.

1913 Dec. 22, Marisol Chantwell dies giving birth to a stillborn son.

1917 Jan. 11, dispatch of the so-called "Zimmerman telegram."

1919 Oct. 18, death of Penwick Gathright.

1936 Apr. 19, death of Granville Gathright. Chester Gathright becomes editor/publisher of the *Silvercliff Bugle.*

1938 July 22, shooting of Benny Compton.

1941 Dec. 7, Japanese forces attack Pearl Harbor; "a date which will live in infamy."

1945 Aug. 6, Barnabus Chantwell, alias Chicken Smith, passes away at the age of 85.

Bob Carlton lives and works in Leander, TX. For those willing to navigate a minefield of broken links and a sea of literary obscurity, more about him and his work can be found at www.bobcarlton3.weebly.com.

Thank you to the Wapshott Press sponsors, supporters, and Friends of the Wapshott Press.

Muna Deriane
Ann Siemens
Suzanne Siegel
Debbie Jones
Steven Acker
Jennifer Bentson
Kathleen Bonagofsky
Carol Colin
Ted Waltz
Cynthia Henderson
Aubrey Hicks
Nancy Lilly
Jeff Morawetz
Patricia Nerad
Amanda Nerad
Elaine Padilla
Bradley Rader
Laurel Sutton
Deana Swart
Kathleen M. Warner

The Wapshott Press is a 501(c)(3) not-for-profit enterprise publishing work by emerging and established authors and artists. We publish books that should be published. We are very grateful to the people who believe in our plans and goals, as well as our hopes and dreams. Our new website is at www. WapshottPress.org